Corpus Delectable

Published in electronic format by
PROLOGUE BOOKS
an imprint of F+W Media, Inc.
10151 Carver Road
Blue Ash, Ohio 45242
www.prologuebooks.com

eISBN 10: 1-4405-3715-1
eISBN 13: 978-1-4405-3715-8
POD ISBN 10: 1-4405-5519-2
POD ISBN 13: 978-1-4405-5519-0

This work has been previously published in print format by:
Pocket Books of Canada, Ltd.

Corpus Delectable

PROLOGUE BOOKS

F+W Media, Inc.

One

She was late.

She'd been a musical voice on the telephone identifying herself as one Jean Putnam. The music had been overlaid with strain and urgency when she'd asked for an immediate appointment.

"I'll detour on my way to the Claverys' party," she'd said. "I can be there in thirty minutes. I've got to see you, Mr. Rivers."

"What about?"

"It's a little complicated to try to explain on the phone. I've got to know whether or not a certain thing is true."

"I'll wait for you," I'd said.

Nearly an hour had passed.

There was nothing else at the moment to keep me in the office. But I decided to give Jean Putnam a little longer. People never call a private detective merely for the exercise of lifting the phone.

Energetic brass-band music filtered into the office from outside. I ambled to the window and idled a few minutes with glimpses of the glittering parade passing the intersection a couple of blocks away. The floats were elegant, the girls gorgeous, the pirates fearsome. The packed masses of spectators over there had a common bond, a carefree, festive spirit.

Tampa, Florida, where I operate, is the only city in the country to be captured every year by pirates. The capitulation is a joyous one. It started back in 1904 when somebody got the happy idea of a fun week dedicated to the legendary José Gaspar, who roamed these Gulf waters back when buccaneers were for real.

The current invasion of Tampa had started this morning, when the three-hundred-ton replica of old José's flagship had sailed into the Hillsborough River, which slices Tampa in half.

Followed by a vast fleet of pleasure boats, the *José Gaspar*'s rigging and masts had swarmed with Florida lovelies and Tampa businessmen in pirate regalia. As the ship had neared downtown Tampa, the cannons had started roaring. Scores of thousands of tourists and Floridians had cheered almost as loudly.

With the ship at dock, Ye Mystic Krewe, as it's dubbed, had poured gaily ashore, brandishing cutlass and pistol. The mayor had issued the proclamation of capitulation to Ye Mystic Krewe, and the Jolly Roger had been run up on the City Hall flagstaff to usher in the week-long wing-ding known as the Gasparilla Festival.

As I turned from the window, nearly a million people heard seventy-six trombones jar the buildings on Franklin Street. The call of the music brought an off-key whistle of accompaniment from me. The building housing my office, on a grubby side street, seemed all the more drab and deserted.

I gave up, let the seventy-six trombones have the field, and wandered to the office doorway, where the lettering reads: NATIONWIDE DETECTIVE AGENCY, *Southeastern Division, Agent in Charge,* ED RIVERS.

I palmed the knob, debating whether or not to close up and join the rest of the building's denizens in the pursuit of piratical pleasures.

I assumed that the Clavery blast, which Jean Putnam

had promised to detour, was one of those endless parties for which Gasparilla provides a unique and offbeat reason. I'd never met or heard of the girl before. For all I knew, she had decided the party wouldn't wait, but the private cop would always be around.

I pushed back my cuff and looked at my watch in its heavy nest of oily-looking hairs. More than an hour now since Jean Putnam's voice had made its thirty-minutes promise.

Give her five more minutes, I thought.

She needed another thirty or forty seconds. As I started to turn back into the office, I gave the corridor a final glance, and she was suddenly there, a still life framed in the stairwell several yards away.

She was a still life that vibrated, like atomic particles molded in about five-six of female perfection. She was dressed in a very fetching pirate costume that accented her firm, flowing, youthful lines. The delicate loveliness of her face was topped by a red silk scarf turbaned on her head. The purposely ragged bottoms of her scarlet pants reached just below the hips. Her legs were bare from that point down to where the black oilcloth boots began.

"Miss Putnam?" I inquired.

She nodded vaguely. Her mouth opened slightly. She still hadn't moved, and a frown crept between my heavy brows.

And a new sensation blew cold across the back of my neck.

I lunged from the doorway. When I was halfway to her, she made a weak gesture toward me. She crumpled and disappeared into the yawning stairwell. She fell with

the cruel sounds of tissue and bone striking uncontroll-
ably against inanimate stairs and iron railing.

I reached the break in the corridor and went down
the stairs skidding on my heels. She was a twisted mass
of creamy flesh and crimson cloth on the landing.

When I reached her and dropped to one knee, I saw
that not all of the redness was in her costume. A bullet
had struck her in the back near her left shoulder blade. It
had angled deep in her body. It hadn't come out through
her right breast, because it had struck bone, ricocheting
briefly inside of her and tearing the hell out of her chest
cavity. Bleeding to death inside, she shouldn't even have
had the strength to drag herself upright in the stairwell.

Turning her, I knew an emergency ambulance ride
wasn't going to help her. The young violet eyes were
already going murky as the life left her.

She was trying to speak. She made little actual
sound, more a suggestion of words. "Are you . . . Rivers?"

No need to tell her to take it easy. She hadn't a clock
tick left.

"Yes," I said. "Who did this to you?"

"Man . . . Strange man . . ."

"Someone hired to do it?"

"Yes . . ."

"Why?"

"I . . . Incense . . ."

It came to her then that she was face to face with
the darkest of all mysteries. She summoned her reserves
to fight it. Her hand clutched my arm. Her mouth twisted
in a frightened, childlike plea for help. A brief fire came
to her eyes. Then she went limp. She was gone.

I let her shoulders slide from my fingers. Over on
Franklin Street, in another world, the seventy-six trom-

bones had passed on, and the mammoth parade continued.

Here, the silence crimped tight with unpleasant meaning. She couldn't have carried the slug far. She must have been okay when she'd come off the street . . .

As I turned from her, a silenced gun burped in the corridor below, and a slug put a neat round in the wall behind my head. I dropped behind a square newel post, reaching for the .38 I carry as a part of my armament. The rest of the equipment consists of a knife in a hidden sheath at the nape of my neck.

I heard his footsteps in the corridor, heavy but fast. Swinging around the newel post, I dropped from the landing.

The second I showed my puss in the lower corridor the silenced gun made another nasty, anti-Rivers sound. I jerked back into the cover of the stairway.

My body felt as if it were smothering in its own sweat. Part of it came from being plain scared, but not all. I wanted a chance to talk back to the crumb's whispering gun with the honestly loud voice of the .38.

I dropped low and plunged across the corridor, ready to fire at anything that moved.

Flattened against the far wall, I jerked some breath into my lungs. The corridor was silent and empty. I shoved myself away from the wall, racing toward the double glass doors.

When I reached the sidewalk, a drum and bugle corps on Franklin Street let go with a concussion that poured through the narrow canyons formed by buildings.

Diagonally across the street from me, I glimpsed movement. I got an impression of a big man wearing a dark-gray suit and coconut straw hat. Then he was out of sight, disappearing into an alley.

Not a pedestrian was in sight. Nothing else moved on the narrow, deserted back street. Cars were parked in every available space. I eeled between a couple of them and ran to the far sidewalk. At the entrance to the alley, I stopped and plastered myself against the corner of the building for a second. I'd have given five bills for the sight of a cop.

Dropping low, I chanced a look in the alley. I saw a parked pickup truck, the usual garbage cans, a loading platform. It was a scene of desertion, of quiet, almost of stark desolation. A few blocks away the multitudes cheered a bathing beauty on a float of flowers.

A drop of sweat came down and stung the corner of my eye. As I eased into the alley, a tightness spread through my chest, transforming the normal act of breathing into a conscious, labored process. My grip on the .38 had the trigger on a hairline.

He wasn't hiding behind the first rack of garbage cans, or the next. The pickup truck was empty, and he wasn't crouched and waiting beyond the loading platform.

The end of the alley was marked by a meeting of sunlight and shadows. I slipped the gun in the side pocket of my suit jacket and padded across to another sidewalk.

I went a block and rounded a corner. Ahead of me was a solid jam of humanity. Over their heads I glimpsed the upper portions of a passing float. A baby was crying fretfully somewhere in the crowd. Cardboard periscopes bobbed up and down. Young daddies stood with kids straddling their shoulders. At first glance I counted a dozen coconut straw hats, like chips floating on a restless sea.

He was under plenty of tension, I reminded myself. I stood in readiness for the natural thing to happen, waiting for one of those hats to turn as the man under it sneaked a glance backward.

A band blaring Sousa strains came and went. On the following float, a tall, leggy girl, gleaming with golden gilt, stood on the back of a golden dolphin, a golden chain in her hand.

The golden image slipped past the edges of my vision. A grinning, gigantic pirate, two stories tall and inflated with helium, floated past the intersection. A troop of cowboys from the Kissimee ranching area clop-clopped by on spirited palomino horses. Another band marched past with drums rattling a swift cadence.

None of the hats had turned. I knew he was a cool, experienced professional. He had to be aware of my presence, but he had the self-discipline to keep from revealing himself.

My hands had gradually become hard knots of frustration. I wheeled abruptly and headed toward my office.

When I got back to Jean Putnam, a glistening green fly had landed on her smooth, firm cheek and was crawling toward the young, innocent mouth. With a thick curse, I shooed the fly away, cut my eyes from her, and hurried up the stairs.

Trying to keep my mind away from the implications attached to the young, cooling body on the stair landing, I phoned police headquarters.

Over a route of back streets, an official contingent made an almost stealthy arrival in about ten minutes. Two cars and a sleek, black Caddy ambulance disgorged tech men, meat-wagon boys, uniformed cops, and Lieutenant Steve Ivey of Homicide.

The preliminaries were quiet, Ivey surveying the girl, murmuring instructions, motioning me back to my office.

A big, bald, placid man, Steve never made headlines. But he was a good detective, making up in integrity and determination what he might have lacked in brilliance. He rested against the edge of my desk patiently while I told him what had happened.

"And you've no inkling why she called, Ed?"

"Only that she wanted a question settled in her mind," I said.

"I wish you'd got a better look at the gunman."

"Look, hell," I said. "I would have guaranteed his medical or funeral expenses for one clean shot at him."

"Know anything about Jean Putnam, Ed? Where she lived? Who her people were?"

"Nothing. I don't even know if she was a Tampa resident. She might have been a nice young secretary from Topeka vacationing here during Gasparilla week."

"Chances are she was local."

"Chances of anything are just about endless at the moment," I said.

"She was single."

"Unless she wasn't as nice and innocent as she looked," I said, "and had shucked her wedding band for some hanky-panky during Gasparilla."

Ivey used a padded handkerchief to wipe moisture from the sweatband of his hat. "A swift, hard strike by a cool gunman . . ." he murmured. "We're reasonably sure of only one thing. It was a professional killing. The toughest kind. He fills his contract. He makes his hit, and this time tomorrow he could be in Gary, Detroit, or L.A."

"I know."

"Except," Ivey said, "I don't think he will be. I think he'll be right here in Tampa, thanks to you."

"Did you have to put it into words?" I said.

"He has no way of knowing how much the girl might have been able to tell you, Ed. A pro killer can't leave loose ends like that."

"The pay-off party won't be happy until the error is fixed," I admitted.

Ivey looked up slowly. The office was very quiet. Steve and I had known each other a long time. "I could put you in protective custody, Ed, or jail you as a material witness."

"For how long?" I asked. "Until the guy dies of old age?"

Ivey sighed heavily. "The idea is full of negative values."

"It leaks negative all over the place, Steve. I should sit in jail while the gunsel regains his balance? While whoever hired him has a chance to mend fences, plan the next move, really set me up? No thanks!"

I stood at the window, looking at the holiday spectacle passing on Franklin Street. A Shriners' band was really giving out with "There'll Be a Hot Time in Old Town Tonight."

I looked at Steve over my shoulder. "I won't be much good in this town if I let a prospective client get knocked off on my doorstep and run and hide. I didn't make the eight ball, Steve, but you add everything up and it looks like I'm right behind it."

"Maybe we can grab our man quick, Ed."

"And supply the pallbearers if you can't," I said. The bitterness in my voice was for real, and Ivey was left without an answer. He looked at me a couple of seconds longer, then punched me on the shoulder and turned to leave.

As he neared the door, he stuck his handkerchief in his pocket and covered his peeled-egg pate with his hat. A coconut straw. In this climate, even cops in plainclothes wear them.

Two

There is always a way.

I picked up the phone book and opened it to the C section. "Clavery" wasn't a common name. I hoped the Clavery throwing the party that had been Jean Putnam's destination didn't have an unlisted phone.

I started dialing.

The first few Claverys didn't answer. Then a salty voice expressed an opinion of people who call a wrong number and wake a night-shift worker in the middle of his bedtime.

I got another Clavery on the line and repeated the question: "Has Jean Putnam got there yet?"

"Who?"

"Jean. She was on her way to your party."

"Party? Ain't no party . . ."

"Sorry," I said. "I dialed the wrong number."

The next-to-last Clavery phone rang three times before

it was picked up. The aloof voice of a trained domestic answered. "The Van W. Clavery residence."

Bursts of laughter, stereo jazz in the background. My hand tightened on the phone.

"Has Miss Jean Putnam arrived?" I asked.

"I haven't seen her, sir. Who is calling? I'll look among the guests if you wish."

"No, don't bother."

"Is there a message?"

"No," I said. "No message."

I hung up, made a note of the address, and left the office.

Located in swank Palma Grande, the Clavery home was a modern architect's dream in glittering glass and concrete. I turned off the wide boulevard and parked behind the string of cars in the driveway.

Walking toward the house, I heard Al Hirt spinning on a turntable and the sounds of bright, gay people beyond the house, on the patio side. I didn't need to see the scene to know it. There'd be a pool out there, tables heavy with food and drink. People mingling or sitting at tables under big beach umbrellas. A few couples dancing. Bikinis and diaper-like trunks on those attracted to the pool. Sprinkled among the swim wear and pirate costumes would be a business suit or two worn by squares destined to leave early.

The party was one of those casual facets of Florida living that begins when somebody announces open house for one reason or another. Today the reason was the start of Gasparilla. Later the blast might splinter itself into scattered restaurants for dinner or descend en masse on a night club late tonight. It would finally peter out in exhaustion.

I made with the chimes button beside the bleached wood door. A trim maid of middle age responded to my summons. She didn't place me as one of the clique. Behind her spectacles, her eyes were cool. "Yes?"

"I'm a friend of Miss Putnam's," I said.

"The gentleman who called?"

"Yes."

"I don't believe she's arrived, sir."

A crisp, female voice behind the maid said, "What is it, Zola?"

"A gentleman looking for Miss Putnam, Mrs. Clavery." The maid moved aside as her employer came to the door.

Mrs. Clavery was a woman of cool, aloof, almost sleek beauty. She was thirty, or forty, or fifty. There was no way of knowing by looking at her. Her face and body had received endless and expensive care during all her years. She had the ageless perfection of a fine painting. Her hair was like polished ebony, and her eyes were so black they looked purple. She wore a polished-cotton print dress with an air of careless sophistication.

"I'm Mrs. Natalie Clavery," she said. "What is this about Jean?"

She'd glanced me over as she spoke. Her eyes recoiled slightly. I didn't mind. A slope-shouldered 190 on a six-foot frame, I have a face that usually brings a reaction. It gives women ideas, hot or cold. It inspires caution or complete trust in men. There seems to be no middle ground, but it's my face, creased, swarthy, thick-skinned, with sleepy brown eyes under hooded lids, and I'm stuck with it.

"My name is Ed Rivers, Mrs. Clavery. I'd like to talk to you."

"About Jean?"

"Yes."

"I don't understand . . . but can't you make it some other time? We're in the midst of a bit of entertaining."

"I'm afraid I'll have to insist," I said. I opened my wallet and showed her the photostat of my license.

She regarded it with some hesitancy but without a change of expression. Still looking at the photostat, she instructed the maid, "Tell Mr. Clavery to come to the study."

Then she stepped aside, made a small motion with her graceful, long-fingered hand. "This way, Mr. Rivers."

I entered a living room that was a sunken garden in which the tricky use of glass gave you the feeling of being outdoors. Following her, I noted the swing of her hips, the flash of her bare, firm calves. Off the top of my mind, I made a guess about her husband. He had himself one hell of a woman—or an icy queen with a firm grip on an invisible ring in his nose. Her decision as to a relationship with a man wouldn't contain reservations. He would be all or nothing.

The study was more bleached wood, floor-length draperies, with pale-tan leather furnishings. She closed the door and leaned against it.

"I can't possibly make a connection between Jean and a private detective, Mr. Rivers."

"Have you known her long?"

"Since she became private and social secretary to Señora Isabella Sorolla y Batione."

"The hefty Spanish monicker strikes a chord," I said.

"The newspapers gave the señora considerable space."

"Yes, I'm beginning to remember. She was an old Venezuelan *doña* who came to Tampa and settled a year or so ago, after Venezuelan terrorists planted a bomb in her husband's office."

"You are correct, Mr. Rivers." Natalie Clavery moved to the desk and chose a cigarette from a beaten silver humidor. "The bomb killed both the husband and the daughter of Señora Isabella. The old lady never wanted to see her native country again."

"And she got her wish," I said. "Didn't she die a few days ago here in Tampa?"

"Yes, of a kidney ailment compounded by a heart attack. But then, none of us lives forever. Señora Isabella had a full measure of years—more than eighty of them."

"What else can you tell me about Jean Putnam?" I asked.

She speared me with an arched brow. "Why should I tell you anything?"

Before I had a chance to answer, the study door opened. The man who entered was lean, wiry, his movements indicative of a quick, nervous energy. His thin face had a harried look reflecting about forty-five years of anxious living. He had thin lips, a sharp nose, intense eyes, and sparse, faded brown hair. Skinny as he was, he somehow looked natural and slightly dangerous in his pirate's costume.

"Van," his wife said quietly, "this man's credentials identify him as Ed Rivers, a private detective."

He cut a glance at her. I sensed a quick understanding between them.

"I see," he said. He extended his hand. "I'm Van Clavery, Mr. Rivers. What can we do for you?"

"He was asking about Jean Putnam," Natalie Clavery said.

"What about her?" he asked.

"I'm afraid she's in trouble."

"Jean? Trouble?" he said, as if the two were totally inconsistent. "I'm sorry to hear it. What kind of trouble? How does it concern us?"

I let his anxious flow of words go unanswered. "Tell me something about her," I suggested.

"A fine girl. A friend. She was employed by a business associate of mine."

"You represent a Batione interest?" I asked.

Clavery nodded, a jerk of the head. "Tropical hardwood timber. I import it. Because of my business association, the old *señora* chose Tampa after her husband and daughter were killed by terrorists in Venezuela. Also, as you know, Ybor City, the Latin Quarter, with its Spanish-speaking population and Old World flavor, differentiates Tampa from all other American cities. The old lady felt more at home here than in any other place in the United States."

"Were you instrumental in Jean's going to work for Señora Isabella?"

"No," he said. "Fred Eppling, the old lady's attorney, suggested the arrangement. But we got to know Jean pretty well during her term of employment."

"Before we continue this," Natalie Clavery said, "I think you should tell us what kind of trouble Jean Putnam is in, Mr. Rivers."

"She's dead," I told them. "Murdered."

There was an absolutely empty second of time during which they did nothing but stare at me. Then Natalie Clavery went white. Her husband clutched the arms of a chair and lowered himself.

"Impossible," he said. "Impossible!"

In a controlled voice, Natalie said, "When?"

"Early this afternoon. She was dressed for your party, intending to detour by my office on the way here."

"How?"

"She was shot," I said.

"Merciful God!" Clavery said. "Who would do that?"

"A man. We think he is a professional hoodlum. He hasn't been identified as yet."

Clavery's hands were hard tentacles of bone on the arms of the chair. "It's senseless! She's the least likely candidate for murder I could name . . ."

Three

"Good background?" I asked.

"Impeccable. Not wealthy, but substantial. Her parents were killed in an accident when Jean was young, but they left enough to see her through school, including an excellent finishing school."

Clavery's growing and suppressed nervousness was reflected in his eyes, in his hands as he knuckled his jaw, curled his fingers to pick an imaginary hangnail. I had the distinct feeling that his mind wasn't really on what he was saying. "Señora Isabella was Jean's first employer. The old lady considered herself lucky to have found such a girl."

"What my husband is trying to say," Natalie said as she broke in, "is that Jean was conscientious, quiet, devoted to her work. She led a sheltered, faultless life, if somewhat dull."

"I'd very much appreciate her address," I said.

"She moved, a couple of days ago, to share an apartment with an one-time schoolmate, Lura Thackery. The address is on Calmwaters Boulevard."

"Where had she lived previously?"

"In Señora Isabella's hacienda," Natalie said. "The old lady provided a very lovely suite, including a room they outfitted and used as an office. Jean moved in at the beginning of her employment. She remained after the *señora*'s death until her duties were completed."

"Catching up tag ends?"

"Something like that," Natalie said. "Señora Isabella had one surviving blood relation, a granddaughter, Elena Sigmon. The old lady's son-in-law, Keith Sigmon, and Elena flew in from Venezuela forty-eight hours after the *señora* died. Elena had never been in the States before. Jean Putnam remained to give whatever assistance she could."

Clavery pushed himself out of the chair as if it had become a pincushion. "Poor Jean! Did she reach you before she died, Rivers?"

"Yes," I said. I didn't elaborate. I let him stew, watching him closely. I sensed the fright in him, rather than seeing any visible evidence of it.

Then Natalie intervened smoothly. "I'm sure Mr. Rivers would acquaint us with anything Jean might have said concerning us."

A look passed between them. It gave Clavery a little more fortitude. With a nervous moistening of his lips, he said, "I wish we could be of more help."

"Don't fret over it," I suggested, certain that he would. "I usually get where I'm going."

I didn't wait to be invited out. I stopped at the first

shopping center I passed and got Lura Thackery's address and phone number from a phone-booth directory. I let the phone ring a dozen times before I decided she wasn't home.

I filed Lura Thackery for future reference, and drove out to Señora Isabella's hacienda.

The local papers had carried a picture-feature spread about the place when the old lady had purchased it from the estate of a one-time citrus magnate.

The old woman had made the restoration of the home and grounds a pet project. She had completely renovated the house. With upwards of twenty million dollars to toy with, she'd brought in artwork from as far away as Valencia and Milan. She'd put a crew of horticulturists at work on the tropical gardens that surrounded the house like a vast, carefully planned, exotic jungle. There were even strange birds of colorful plumage at home in the foliage that shaded the long, winding drive and acres of green lawn and flower beds.

The house slid into my view, a huge square U of stucco, stone, and iron filigree. Vaulted open porticoes with slim columns faced inward on a flagstoned courtyard where a fountain played over lily pads in a marble pool.

The aura of Castilian refinement was shattered by a female voice screeching a stream of curses in Spanish. A man's voice told her in everyday American that if she didn't shut up he would knock her damned teeth out.

I broke into the cozy family discussion by lifting and lowering the heavy brass knocker on a massive wormy cypress door.

The heavy portal was opened by a girl in a scanty pirate's costume. Deeply tanned, she had a lean-hipped, small-breasted figure that suggested sly sensuality. Her face was small; in later years it would be the face of a vixen; right now it was startlingly pretty, with a mouth that was almost too wide, a small nose, and wide-set blue eyes under carelessly unplucked brows. A wisp of dark-blond hair showed beneath the bandanna knotted on her small head, and in her right ear she wore a large ring of gold.

As she focused her eyes on my face, I realized she was in the first warm, cozy stage of drunkenness. "What is it?"

"Are you Miss Sigmon? Miss Elena Sigmon?"

"Uh-huh. Who are you?"

"My name is Ed Rivers."

"Whatever you're selling, we don't want any."

"I'm not selling anything. I want to talk to you," I said.

"Make an appointment. I'm on my way to a party."

"It's about a girl who worked for your grandmother," I said. "Jean Putnam."

"She no longer lives here. She moved out a couple of days ago."

Elena Sigmon tried to close the door. My shoulders were in the way. The alcoholic haze lessened in her eyes. "You seem to be a ruffian," she said thinly. "Do you want me to call the police?"

"If you like."

She regarded me with eyes that had become surly and brooding. Then she eased the pressure against the door. "Do explain yourself as briefly as possible. My day is already behind schedule."

I was in an entry foyer that was austere, almost barren. Ahead, a short stairway dropped to a living room the size of a small cathedral with a vaulted ceiling. "So is Jean," I said. "Considerably behind."

"Really? What is she to you?"

"A client."

"Are you a lawyer?"

"No," I said. "A private detective."

A momentary chill came to her. "I think you had better talk to Keith, my father." She turned with the lean motions of a lithe, sinewy female leopard and went out of sight in the spacious living room.

She either had trouble finding him, or they carried on a conversation of nearly ten minutes' duration. When Elena finally returned with him, Keith Sigmon greeted me with a smile and outstretched hand.

He was a tall, slender, slightly dissipated man of about forty-five. Age, and probably his habits, were just beginning to mar a lean face chiseled in lines of classic good looks. His jaw line was clean, his chin square. His lips, nose, and widow's-peaked forehead were patrician in cut and perfectly blended. His black hair, barely salted with gray, seemed molded in softly waving lines to his proud head. "I'm Keith Sigmon, Mr. Rivers, and hope I may be of service to you."

With a motion of his hand, he invited me into the living room. "Elena, why don't you get Mr. Rivers a drink?"

"Anything you'd prefer?" She was now the dutiful daughter. Her attitude had veered toward warmth.

"I'll pass," I said.

Sigmon patted her shoulder. "Then get me a small Bacardi, dear."

The living room interested me only because Jean Putnam had lived and worked here. Sigmon noted my survey of the substantial furnishings, the Persian carpeting, the fine oil paintings on the walls. The room reflected real grace and luxury, the sort of good taste that is generations in the making, none of the tinsel or gaudiness of the newly rich.

"I see you appreciate my mother-in-law's eye for quality," Sigmon said. "She will be missed, not only by those close to her. There are few of her breed left in the world."

Sigmon was now quite a contrast to the male voice that had threatened dental destruction to a brattishly screeching daughter.

"I'm under the impression," I said, "that Señora Isabella was quite fond of Jean Putnam. Maybe the old lady recognized points of breeding they had in common."

"I really couldn't say. Neither can I understand why Jean has sent a private detective here."

"We're retained for various reasons," I said. "Sigmon . . . Not a Venezuelan name, is it?"

"American, as a matter of fact." His voice took on an edge.

"Do you get back often?"

"I haven't been back since I chose Venezuela many years ago, Mr. Rivers. I would not be back now if Señora Isabella were still alive."

"I suppose you've found a lot of changes in the United States."

"I really haven't been interested."

"When did you get in?"

"On Tuesday, following my mother-in-law's death. Fred Eppling, the attorney, cabled the news. Elena drove from Caracas to the mountain cottage where I was vacationing and told me what had happened. The next day we flew from Caracas to Mexico City and jetted across the Gulf to Tampa."

"Known Eppling long?"

His shortening temper thinned his lips. "I don't understand the purpose or the necessity for this cross-examination, Rivers. But I don't mind answering your questions, in exchange for a few answers from you."

"Eppling," I reminded.

"He entered the picture after Elena's grandmother left Venezuela and found need of a legal adviser here. I introduced myself to him when he met our plane."

"Was Jean Putnam with him?"

Sigmon shook his head. "I met her that evening. She was here at the house, staying on to put her work in final order."

Elena returned with that leopardine flow of motion. She had two drinks in her hands. She gave one to her father. "If the party is out, I'm going to get drunk, Papa dear. Rivers, you're a big, ugly, strangely attractive man. And it's Gasparilla, or haven't you heard? Why not take the afternoon off and let me show you how to get drunk? I'll bet we could make Cloud Nine music, drunk together."

She had nipped heavily while fixing the drinks for herself and Dad. The fog was back in her eyes, heavier than ever. She wasn't too drunk to know, dimly, what she was saying—merely too drunk to really care.

Sigmon went white with fury. He raked her with his gaze. She was standing in an attitude of abandonment, in a slouch that thrust her crotch forward. In two generations, the old *señora*'s breeding had degenerated to animal vulgarity.

All of us turned as the heavy knocker boomed on the front door.

Elena waggled a finger. "I'll see who it is, Pops. May be a descendant of José Gaspar who'll drag me off to a nice, hot party."

I thought for a second that Keith Sigmon was going to slap her. Instead, he stood quivering, hands clenched at his sides, as Elena wavered toward the front door.

The caller was a neat, smallish, sandy man dressed quietly in a conservative, expensive business suit. He came briskly toward me. "Fred Eppling," he introduced himself. "You're Ed Rivers, aren't you?"

He had a lean handshake that hinted at considerable tensile strength. The only hint of his age was in the gray at his temples. His eyes, like his body, were quick and ready. I suspected that he'd be right at home on a yacht deck in bad weather.

"You know this man?" Sigmon said.

"Rivers is practically a Tampa institution. He makes the papers now and then." He looked at me earnestly. "You're staying with it?"

"I don't have much choice."

"Staying with what?" Keith Sigmon said.

"Jean Putnam's murder," Eppling said. "I just came from police headquarters, where I talked with Steve Ivey, a homicide detective. It seems that Rivers barely missed sharing a headline with Jean."

Sigmon had an empty-eyed moment of absolute disorientation. Elena hiccuped, a drunken little sound of fright.

Then Sigmon's eyes became quite cold. "So that's why you were nosing around here."

"I imagine Rivers will be sticking his nose in many places," Eppling said as if he were secretly relieved.

"You sonofabitch!" Sigmon said to me.

"Easy on the language, friend. I've taken a natural aversion to you, too."

He looked at my face, took a step back, got his anger under partial control. "Okay Rivers," he said between his teeth. "I've dealt with your breed before. If you're trying to hatch a shakedown, you'll find it damned unhealthy sitting on the nest."

"I didn't lay the eggs, and it wasn't my choice to keep them warm."

Fred Eppling's eyes glinted with pleasure as he watched Sigmon sweat. He shared my lack of respect for the client he had inherited.

"Keith," the attorney said mildly, "why don't you have a drink?"

"An excellent idea," Elena said. "How many shall I mix?"

"Three," Sigmon said. "Rivers is leaving—unless he wants to get arrested for trespassing."

Eppling strolled with me to the door. Silently he handed me one of his business cards. "You won't need an appointment," he said.

"Were you close to Jean Putnam?"

"No, but I respected her. I knew the attorney who was her guardian and the administrator of her estate. He was an old man, died a year ago. Through him, I met Jean."

"Who had a reason to kill her?" I asked.

"No one. Her character was spotless."

"Until," I said, "a tragedy-ridden old lady from Venezuela died."

Four

A bold-breasted, leggy woman in a simple sleeveless white dress was waiting beside my car.

Sunlight glinted on dark-blond hair that spilled to her wide shoulders. At my approach she took off heavy, dark sun glasses. The lustiness extended to her face, with its high cheekbones and strong features.

"You're Ed Rivers, aren't you?"

I nodded.

"My name is"—she made a slight face—"Myrtle Higgins. A little cruel of my parents, don't you think?"

With all those accessories, she should have been a real eye-knocker. Somehow, for no reason I was able to pin down, she just missed the achievement of rare beauty. It wasn't a promise still in her future. While young, she was right now in the full bloom of maturity. She was like a lush fruit which, when touched, is found to be made of wax. Or like a painting by an artist who has mastered all the mechanical details without being able to fuse them into a potential whole.

"What can I do for you, Miss Higgins?"

"I overheard a few words of what went on in the house. I'd like to talk to you."

"Any time."

"How about now?"

"Fine," I said.

She glanced toward the sprawling hacienda. "But not here."

I opened the car door, and she got in without hesitation. I went around the car and slid under the wheel.

I turned the key in the ignition. "Any place in particular?"

"I was invited to a party at the Clavery house."

"I know where it is." I started the car from the driveway.

"I came by here, intending to pick up a few things and take a taxi." She looked back at the house as the man-made jungle closed around us. "I can get my things later. What I overheard . . . it made a couple of uniforms and a pair of whites unimportant."

"You worked for Señora Isabella?"

"Yes. I was her nurse."

"Then you knew Jean Putnam."

"Oh, yes." She hesitated, experiencing difficulty in laying the words out blunt and cold. "Is it true . . . Jean is dead?"

"I'm afraid so."

She opened the wind-vent window wider and let the breeze strike her face. "How did Jean die?"

"She was shot."

A shiver crossed Myrtle Higgins' fine, wide shoulders.

I briefed Myrtle on the rest of it. "And all I get on Jean Putnam is a report of undiluted purity."

"You get the truth, Ed. But Jean was no prig. She was always ready for fun—up to a point. The kind who'd attend the Clavery blast and cut out before the ball turned into a brawl. She was good-natured, sensitive, very considerate."

"Were you close friends?"

"No," Myrtle said. "Friends, compatible co-workers here at the old *señora*'s hacienda. But not bosom pals.

Jean liked people, was friendly with everyone. She'd lived a rather lonely life as an orphan in private schools."

"Do you know a girl named Lura Thackery?"

"Not well," Myrtle said. "But from the way Jean spoke of her, Lura was her closest friend."

"Where's the sense of it?" I said. "Jean was a veritable angel, but a pro killer guns her down like the sluttiest moll about to squeal on the gang."

"From what you say, Ed, she didn't have much time for squealing."

"She said one thing."

"About the theft?" Myrtle asked.

My ears got long and pointed. "Which theft?"

"Was there more than one?"

"Which one are you referring to?" I countered.

"Señora Isabella's old portfolio," Myrtle said. "Jean discovered it missing and told Keith Sigmon about it a couple days ago. He said the brief case contained nothing more than a few personal items of the old lady's, sort of keepsakes. A few snapshots, clippings from newspapers when the *señora*'s husband and daughter were killed —the sort of junk a little old lady will squirrel away."

"Nothing of value?"

"Not that I know of."

"Did Sigmon report the theft?" I asked.

"To the police? I don't think so. He said it wasn't important, that Jean probably had misplaced the portfolio and that it would turn up."

"Has it?"

Myrtle shrugged. "How would I know? Keith Sigmon doesn't confide in me. Anyway, I'm all through at the hacienda, as soon as I move my things to my apartment."

"You don't care much for Keith Sigmon, do you?"

"Frankly, no."

"What do you know about him, Myrtle?"

"Not much. I understand he drifted into Venezuela years ago, met the old *señora*'s daughter, an only child, and eloped with her."

"Fortune hunter?" I suggested.

"Could be. Señora Isabella hated his guts. She no longer had to tolerate him, after a terrorist's bomb killed her husband and daughter, Keith's wife."

"Which explains why she left Sigmon behind when she fled Venezuela," I said. "But Elena stayed in Venezuela too, don't forget."

"Maybe Papa Keith influenced his daughter's decision, Ed."

"Sure," I said, "Elena being the only remaining string Papa had on the fabulous fortune."

The Clavery house came into view. The number of parked cars had increased. I eased into the driveway.

"As the old *señora*'s nurse," I said, "you should know if there was any remote possibility that she didn't die from natural causes."

Myrtle gave me a glance. "None, Ed. Absolutely none. She had the best doctors attending her. You could check with them."

She stirred as I stopped the car in the middle of the driveway. "Actually, I think a terrorist's bomb helped shorten the old lady's life, Ed. Except for a sort of dutiful affection for Elena, she'd lost everything dear to her. She went through the motions of keeping herself feverishly interested in a lot of projects, but it was a cover-up. The *señora* never got over the tragedy, the moment the bomb exploded. Finally she admitted to herself that she was old, sick, and tired. In the end, she quit fighting, Ed."

I watched the lithe movements of Myrtle as she got out of the car. I had a hunch as to what was needed to put the spark in all that potential loveliness.

"Thanks for the lift, Ed." She closed the door and stood looking at me a moment.

"If I have more questions," I said, "where do I ask them?"

"I've told you everything I know."

"But I'm pretty good at thinking up questions."

A smile came to her wide red lips. "I'm not in the phone book yet."

"I'll try information," I said.

"You'd find a clue." She turned and moved away from the car toward the noise that all those pleasure-seeking pirates were making.

I spent the brief remainder of the afternoon at police headquarters, joining Lieutenant Steve Ivey in his routine. His men were rounding up known gunsels and questioning stoolies.

The net result was zero. If the Unknown Party under the coconut straw hat was local, nobody was talking.

When I came out of headquarters, the day had turned to a short semi-tropical twilight. The twilight had deepened to darkness by the time I worried the car through massed traffic toward my apartment on the edge of the Cuban quarter, Ybor City.

I parked the heap in the long, shedlike garage behind the beat-up old building, got out, and arched my back muscles. I was dogged. Everywhere there were bright lights and frolicsome people, but for me it was the low, tag end of a depressing day.

I went across the street to a narrow stool-and-counter eatery and knocked the edge off fatigue with a thick Cuban sandwich and a beaker of suds.

I thought of Jean Putnam's young face with the light going out of it. It reminded me somehow of a face I'd known long ago, years ago. I—and the world—had been young then.

She'd been mine, the girl with that other face. Or so I'd thought. I'd known her in Jersey, where I had been born, grown up, walked my first beat as a rookie cop. I had never been able to figure the mystery of her. She had run off with a punk I was trying to nail, and their car had tried, and failed, to beat a fast freight train to a crossing.

With the flowers fresh on her grave, I had drunk to her memory. I hadn't quit drinking, not for a long time— not until the day I woke up in a back alley right here in Ybor City. I'd lain there with the sweat hot and cold on me, the searing sun in my eyes, and I'd realized I would never completely burn the memory of her out of me.

I'd got a job on the docks of Port Tampa and worked the rotgut out of my system. Nationwide Detective Agency had given me a second chance. I'd been with the outfit ever since, more than sixteen years now.

And today another face of innocence had looked into my life, and I wondered if I would ever solve the mystery of this one either....

When I came out of the beanery, the very air of the Quarter seemed to quiver with a feeling of festivity. The crowds were laughing, filled with Gasparilla friendliness. Jalopies piled with boys and girls mingled with the sleek, purring limousines of the Latin elite. In the gay garb of old Spain, *caballeros* and *señoritas* were on their way to torchlighted street dances that marked the annual fun festival.

The narrow streets with their shops and stalls and lacy iron balconies shimmered with light, resounded with gay voices. Ragged kids, infected by the general excitement, dropped sputtering firecrackers behind passers-by and ducked into alleys in Spanish-shrilling gangs.

I jostled my way into a sidewalk phone booth. I slugged the phone and tried the number of Jean Putnam's one-time classmate, Lura Thackery.

By the fifth or sixth ring, I'd decided the girl with whom Jean had shared an apartment was still out. Probably enjoying Gasparilla, unaware that Jean was dead.

I gave the phone a couple more chances. I was hanging up on the final ring when a connection was made. A girl's voice answered, breathlessly, as if she'd heard the phone and rushed into her apartment.

"Miss Thackery?" I asked.

"Yes."

"My name is Rivers," I said.

"Rivers? I'm afraid I don't know you," she said, too quickly.

"I'd like to come over. I have something relating to Jean Putnam I must discuss with you."

"I'm very busy . . ."

"I'll have to insist, Miss Thackery. It's urgent."

"Are you . . ." she hesitated, "the man Jean was going to see?"

"Yes."

"Is she with you now?"

"No, Miss Thackery. I'm afraid she isn't. I have the address. I'll be right over."

Five

She was trying, not very successfully, to hide her agitation as she showed me into the small, tasteful apartment on Calmwaters Boulevard. She was a thin girl with an angular figure like a *Vogue* model. I don't make a habit of reading *Vogue,* but she wasn't unattractive, if you like them without meat.

She turned and faced me squarely for the first time. Her features were fine-boned, almost delicate. Her skin had a gently transluscent quality on the surface. She had a wide, sensitive mouth and very arresting eyes. Eyes of the deepest blue, set in misty hollows. I sensed that she was the kind of girl who could weep softly over the images evoked by a tender, tragic little poem.

Her slender hands reminded me of the subtle twitching of a butterfly's wings when the insect is at rest.

"When may I expect Jean, Mr. Rivers?"

I took her hands and pressured her gently into a chair. Those large, haunting eyes lifted to make a study of me. The silence began to fill the apartment like a creeping fog. Lura Thackery wasn't repelled by my face; she seemed suddenly to need the strength she saw there.

"Is she badly hurt, Mr. Rivers?" she said at last.

"Yes."

"She won't be coming back at all, will she?"

"No," I said.

The translucence of her face turned to wax. I decided

she needed a sip of water, or something stronger, if I could find it.

When I started to pull away, she gripped my hand tightly in refusal. Her nails dug into my skin as if I were her link with reality right now.

"I told Jean it was none of her business!"

"Do you know why she was coming to see me?" I asked.

"No," she said with a shake of her head that spilled the baby-fine, short-cut brown hair about her forehead and temples.

She recoiled slightly when her eyes met mine. "Why are you looking at me like that?"

"I don't think you're leveling with me, Miss Thackery."

"But I am! Jean said she was going to see a private detective named Rivers. She wanted to explain, but I wouldn't let her. I didn't want to know her reasons!"

Sobs began shaking her body like a sheaf of straw exposed to a cold, hard wind. "What will I do without Jean?" she moaned.

I vaguely pitied and was repelled by her words. Lura was interpolating Jean Putnam's death in terms of her own needs.

"You might think of doing something about her," I said.

She shook her head, writhing in the chair as if the full horror were just now sinking in.

"You don't understand," she said. "Jean was a friend I can never replace. My parents . . . they hated each other. Neither wanted me. Divorced and chasing their own empty, foolish desires, they pretended I didn't exist by placing me in school. I wanted to kill myself—until I met dear, kind Jean."

She mashed her knuckles against her mouth, shutting off the flow of words for a minute.

Her shoulders gradually straightened. Her voice lowered its pitch. "You don't understand, do you? You've a revealing face. You're cruel enough to live in a cruel world. You've never needed people, been lonely, known bitterness or fear."

"No, honey," I said. "Some of us have it perfect."

"Please don't mock me. I can't stand to be mocked or turned away from!"

"I'm sorry," I said. And I really meant it. She couldn't help the way she was put together, any more than the rest of us. How was I to know how much she'd struggled to change herself?

It was no trick to get her to talk, on subjects of her choosing. Her heart broke with nostalgia as she told me how Jean had introduced her to a world in which there was fun, boys, dates for Saturday afternoon football games, occasional dances.

In many close friendships, I reflected, there is a leader, a follower. Lura Thackery had been Jean Putnam's devoted follower, aping her in manner and dress, content to let Jean run interference and carry the ball at the same time.

Her reminiscence included the tale of an afternoon class-cutting so that she and Jean could secretly meet a couple of college boys. The date had included a late evening at a roadhouse strictly off-limits for students at the girls' school.

I assumed it was the wildest and most daring escapade

of Lura Thackery's young life. She'd treasure it as some men secretly delight in a wartime experience.

"Jean was happy as an employee of Señora Isabella, wasn't she?" I suggested, trying to steer the talk.

"Oh, yes."

"The *señora* was a fine old lady, from all I've heard. She really can't be blamed for feeling as she did about Keith Sigmon, her son-in-law."

I'd touched vitriol. It showed in Lura Thackery's expressive eyes. "That rotter!" I was certain that Lura and Jean had gossiped about the rotter.

"Women?" I suggested.

"A parade of them, to repeat gossip. Once he latched onto the old *señora*'s daughter and got himself in a plush spot, Keith Sigmon let his true nature show."

"Then the old lady's daughter and Sigmon weren't happy?"

"Not at all," Lura said. "But his wife's religion was against divorce. After Elena was born, Sigmon felt he was securely tied to the Sorolla y Batione fortune. He took almost openly to the role of a Caracas playboy. Why, at the time the old *señora* died . . ."

"Yes, Lura?"

"From talk that Jean overheard . . . she got the impression that Elena was alone in Caracas when she received news of her grandmother's death. Keith and a girl named Ginny Jameson were—shacked up, I believe is the word—in a mountain cottage. Not very nice for a girl Elena's age, was it? To have to seek out her father in such circumstances at a moment of bereavement . . ."

"This have to do with Jean's appointment with me?"

"I don't know," Lura said.

"When Jean died, she murmured one word. 'Incense.' Mean anything to you?"

"No."

"Jean discovered the disappearance of an old brief case belonging to Señora Isabella. She mention that?"

Lura started to speak; then a stricken look came to her eyes. "You're being dishonest," she accused. "You don't have any real regard for Jean or me. You're trying to pick me, use me!"

"And help you if I can."

She stood up. "You'd better go. And you can help me most by keeping your visit here confidential."

"You know," I said, "the sand starts to smother, if you bury your head too deep. Somebody besides me might decide you know more than you're telling."

"No, no! I've done nothing to get hurt, and I don't intend doing anything. I don't know the answers you're after, I tell you!"

"Very well. Have it your way, Lura."

I started to turn toward the door. She caught my hand. "Why do you want to frighten me?"

"I don't," I said. "I'm merely telling you that you can trust me."

"I haven't found it a very trustworthy world, Mr. Rivers. When one's own parents . . ."

"But you're a grown-up woman now," I said. "No matter how callous your parents were, you're old enough to realize they were, after all, individuals with weaknesses like the rest of us. They probably never realized what they were doing to you."

Her lips curled. "I've heard that kind of talk before."

"You should listen."

"So spake a psychiatrist once," she said bitterly. "It cut no ice, made no difference."

"I'll leave my card," I said. "You can get in touch with me if you change your mind."

"I won't," she said.

"You never know. Anyway, you're going to have to talk to the police."

"I'll tell them the same thing I've told you, Mr. Rivers. I'm not in it. It's not my fight. I won't become involved."

"So much for friendship," I said. "So much for Jean Putnam."

I went to the door and let myself out. Behind the closed door, a desolate, lonely child began weeping in guilt, terror, and despair.

The old building where I live was, as always, a bit musty, bone-dry from years of baking in the endless sun, the lingering smell of spicy Cuban cooking in the dim hallways. I went up to my apartment on the second floor and keyed the door open. Inside, I reached for the light switch beside the door. When I clicked the switch, nothing happened. The room remained gloomy, lighted only by the faint street glow that filtered in.

The breath gusted out of me. Before I could move, a cool circle of metal touched the back of my neck.

"It's hair-triggered, friend," he said softly.

Six

"That's fine," he added, "you're smart not to move a muscle. But now you can. The arm muscles, friend. Easy and slow. Lock the fingers behind the head."

The pressure of the gun barrel faded as he eased safely back. I made motions with the numbness of my arms and twined the fingers at the back of my neck. "Who are you?"

"Little Jack Horner, friend, waiting in a corner, after I found a handy fire-escape window."

"You did a thorough job on Jean Putnam," I said.

"Not thorough enough. Not fast enough. Not the kind of job I like to do, friend, and usually do."

"Would it make any difference to tell you that Jean Putnam didn't have time to say anything?"

"She reached you, friend. She had time."

"She didn't talk," I said.

"Maybe she didn't make sense because you haven't added her up yet."

"But she didn't speak, I tell you!"

"What else could you say, friend?" he asked with a sigh.

Little tics of feeling were returning to my arms and knees. "You'll never get out of the building."

"Come on, now," He laughed softly. "This is the time of gay Gasparilla. Nobody's paying any attention to what happens in this tired old building."

"You got it all figured," I said.

"Sure. It's my turn now, friend. You missed your turn today when the big opening parade was passing on Franklin Street. I knew you were behind me in the crowds, waiting for one of those hats to turn and tip you that a nervous guy was under it. But I don't get nervous, friend."

"Just an old pro."

"Not so old. But I know my business. You muff a turn, friend, you don't get another."

The snout of the gun prodded my back, pushing me a few feet deeper in the room.

"What's it going to look like?" I asked.

"You really want to know?"

"Why not?"

"How about an ordinary accident in the bathtub, friend? You slip, crack your head, and drown. I lay the gun against your skull, strip you down, lay you out in the tub like Sleeping Beauty, and start the water. You won't feel a thing after the first bust on the head, friend. You've been hit on the head before."

My body stiffened, started to turn. The gun jabbed me hard, making me wince.

"Or I can make it tough," he said quietly. "Gut-shoot you, but good. It don't make much difference to me. Because you're for free, friend. Understand? After the first kill, the rest are all for free. You kill one or a hundred, they can only burn you once. It's like you got a license."

The bathroom doorway was a dark rectangle in the gloom. Doorway to a grave.

He was cool, confident, taking his time, letting me cover the last few feet of my life under my own power.

He knew there was no chance of dropping my laced fingers from the nape of my neck and pulling a gun before a silenced slug broke my spine. He had figured all the angles known to him.

But history and cemeteries are full of wise punks. At the base of my neck, my fingers had inched down. They touched the flat handle of the razor-sharp blade sheathed at my nape.

I didn't want to do it. I was so scared my spit glands had dried up.

I steeled myself with a clinching argument: Rivers, what have you got to lose?

As the knife slid free, I threw myself down and to one side. A man of experience, he didn't let the move rattle him. He was prepared. He danced backward to give himself room, to ensure himself from any flailing arms or legs. He thought he was still in control and had plenty of time.

"Okay," he said quietly. He was swinging the gun with deliberate care, intending to make his first shot the last one.

My arm was snapping forward the second my body hit the floor. I didn't expect the throw to be perfect. I was depending on the instinctive reaction of my screwed-tight nerves and muscles. I needed luck.

He didn't know the knife existed until it glinted at him in the gloom. His startled cry mingled with the raw sound of the blade driving hungrily into flesh, blood, and bone high on his left shoulder.

He was briefly rattled, finally. As the blade hit him, his trigger finger reacted. The slug knocked splinters in my face.

I'd rolled right on into the bathroom. I pulled upright, my side pressing against the covering protrusion of the door jamb. The .38 was a comforting weight in my hand.

We waited, he in the bed-sitting room, me in the john, the door frame separating us. From the street came the faint echoes of a strolling orchestra playing a gay Spanish melody.

"Friend," I mimicked, "I got all night."

His silenced gun made a muffled handclap. Paint sprayed from the edge of the door casing.

"I don't mind," he said almost gently. "I'm getting paid for overtime."

"You can talk about it with the Homicide lieutenant who's coming over to discuss the Jean Putnam case."

"You can't bug me, friend."

"I'm not trying," I said. "Stick around and see." Strangely, I'd never before noticed how cramped, small, and smotheringly hot the bathroom really was.

"If anybody was coming, friend, you wouldn't talk about it. Nobody's coming. Just you and me, shut away from a world that's having fun."

His words almost covered the faint protest of a door hinge. I realized he'd used his voice to cover the sound of careful movement.

I peeled around the bathroom door frame. Nothing happened. I rushed across the bed-sitting room toward the closed hallway door. My hand stabbed at the door almost before I thought.

But without touching anything I jerked my hand back as if the doorknob were hot. Flicking a handkerchief from my pocket, I draped the knob, then touched the cloth with the tips of my fingers to open the door.

The corridor was empty. I took the stairs down to the vestibule two at a time. On the front stoop I stopped short, looking at the street.

For a second I had a reasonless hatred for Gasparilla and all the fun connected with it. I wanted to shout down the noisy crowds whose numbers concealed a murderer.

Angrily, my eyes swept the scene for a man I'd never really seen. Then I wheeled about, hurried up to the apartment. Leaving the door open, I jerked up the phone and dialed police headquarters.

The on-duty sergeant jacked in the switchboard. Trying to keep the shakes out of my voice, I briefed him on what had happened. He had it on short wave by the time I'd replaced the phone.

Waiting for them, I moved restlessly, slid a chair under the lighting fixture, mounted it and tightened the bulb he'd loosened.

He was inclined to planning and carrying out his plans in cut-and-dried fashion, the Unknown Party. He didn't like to improvise. Both times, when he'd had to improvise, he'd made his exit.

As I stepped off the chair, somebody punched the buzzer button in the vestibule. I went to the top of the stairs and looked down. I saw the bold, voluptuous lines of Myrtle Higgins in the vestibule.

She came up the stairs slowly. The dim lighting in the hallway lent her a touch of mystery that for a moment deepened all those surface qualities into near loveliness.

"You didn't keep your promise and call information," she said.

"Come in, and I'll give you my excuses."

"During Gasparilla, there are excuses for dashing a poor girl's hopes?"

I took her arm and steered her into the apartment. "Don't touch the doorknob," I said. "A man had to grab it and I'm curious to see what he left."

She gave me a sharp look. "What are you talking about, Ed? What's wrong with you? Aren't you glad to see me?"

"Very glad." I meant it. Myrtle Higgins was a smooth, ivory candle with a wick that needed a flame to transform it. I'm male, and human. I sensed what it would be like, and I wondered if I was the man who could spark the flame.

She crinkled her nose. "What's that smell?"

"I'm afraid it's burned gunpowder."

She looked at me quickly. "You mean the kind that makes bullets?"

"It wasn't popcorn."

"Ed, I don't know if I should be fooling around with you. I thought the murderer was after Jean Putnam, not you. What are you, a walking time bomb?"

Homicide Lieutenant Steve Ivey had phrased it differently. But "rat bait" or "time bomb," it added to the same, and I decided not to talk Myrtle into sticking around against her will.

She seemed to sense my attitude. She thought the whole thing over for a full minute. Then a challenging smile touched her lips. "Maybe I like excitement—and you're prepared if he tries to come back, aren't you?"

"I won't make any rash promises," I said.

"Okay, so the decision is mine alone." She looked me over slowly from head to foot. "I think I'll stick around."

We both turned as heavy footsteps clumped up the stairs. Lieutenant Steve Ivey had been called from his dinner. He headed a small phalanx of people from headquarters.

There was grave concern on Ivey's full, bulldoggish face, and not for having missed his meal. "Are you okay, Ed?"

"Thanks to nobody but myself," I said. "The bait was here. The rat came. The trap didn't spring."

"You get a look at him?"

"Even less than the last time. Do you know Miss Higgins?"

Ivey took off his coconut straw, exposing the creamy globe of his bald pate. "Hello there," he said.

"Hi," Myrtle said. She seated herself on the edge of the daybed that also served as a couch here in the bed-sitting room.

To me, she added, "I met the lieutenant this afternoon."

"We're trying hard for leads, Ed," Steve said. "Talking with everybody connected with Jean Putnam. She, and Miss Higgins here, both worked for Señora Isabella Sorolla y Batione, who died just a———'

"I know," I said. "I'm not Samson—and I was hoping for more action and less jawbone of the ass."

A young plainclothes dick named Gonzales crowded behind Ivey. "You know our problems, Ed."

I let out a sigh. "Sure," I said. "And recriminations won't catch the punk."

I looked past Gonzales' wiry stature to Carruthers. "You bring your pinky powder?"

"Ed, you know I'm addicted to the stuff." Carruthers

had an accent as thick as boiled sorghum. He and Gonzales as kids had gone to the same public schools, but you'd never believe it, listening to the contrast in the way they talked.

I walked to the hallway door.

"The punk had to take a good, firm grip on the doorknob," I told Carruthers. "You keep the thought in mind that I damn near paid with my life for the fingerprints on that knob."

Renewed interest jolted through the room like an electric current.

"Good going, Ed," Ivey said. "If a yegg handles air, Carruthers is the guy to lift the prints."

"Fine," I said. "If the prints are on file. If the punk has ever been printed."

The Rivers-apartment phase of the investigation fanned through the bed-sitting room and bathroom while Carruthers knelt almost reverently at the doorknob. He opened his black bag, started taking out phials and liquids and powders, squares of paper and camel's hair brushes. He carried more junk than an old-time peddler.

Myrtle watched as I recounted my experience to Ivey. It was all taken down by Perone, while Morgan carefully extracted the slug from the framing of the john door.

As Ivey departed with his crew, I followed him to the door.

"You may have given us something concrete," Steve said. "Carruthers is wallowing in prints off the doorknob. Yours are on file, along with your gun permit and license. Needless to say, I'll phone the minute we know anything." He moved to the top of the stairs, paused with his hand on the bannister.

"Ed . . . I'm thankful you were carrying the knife."

"I'm a little happy about it myself. Good night, Steve."

I closed the door behind officialdom and moved toward the daybed.

Myrtle sighed. "You're having a lousy Gasparilla, Ed."

"Let's brighten it up."

"Why not? You look like you need a drink. I know I do."

"I'm a beer man," I said, "but I sometimes have a bottle around."

I went in the kitchenette, scrounged up a nearly full fifth. I poured tall ones. Myrtle and I drank. The smell of gunpowder faded from the apartment. Myrtle wore a musty kind of perfume.

She turned on the clock radio, tuning in soft music.

"Much better than the crowds, Ed," she said, settling herself on the couch.

"I think so."

"Why don't you get out of this Putnam thing?"

"Not a chance. I'm in too deep."

She took my hand, pulled me down beside her. "You could take a little trip."

"And start looking for another job?"

"All right, then," she said almost angrily. "Pour me another drink."

We lowered the level of the fifth considerably. Humming softly, she began unbuttoning my shirt. I didn't protest.

With the shirt peeled off, she seemed to like the sight of sloping shoulders. She tickled the brown mat on my chest. Then she stood up.

"Stretch out," she said, "on your stomach."

"Yes, nurse."

I obeyed the order. Her fingers came down as light as feathers, trailing across my back. She knew how to soothe away the kinks from a long, hard day. I grunted in pure comfort as she began kneading the muscles on my upper arms, across my shoulders.

Her fingers got stronger, becoming urgent. As a masseuse, she became less professional, but much more interesting.

I rolled onto my back, looking at her. The dark-blond hair was loose about her cheeks. The component parts of her hadn't fused. There was still something missing. But she was beautiful enough.

I slid my fingers into the light coppery hair and pulled her face down toward me. With my other hand I tipped her full-featured face so that the light knocked the shadows from it. The surface, physical perfection remained a shell.

"Why do you look at me like that, Ed?"

"It bugs me," I said.

"What does?"

"Something we needn't talk about." I pulled her face down to mine to make contact. "We needn't talk at all." And we didn't. Her lips were too hot for words.

Seven

Some time later, the phone rang. I growled in my throat, padded to the phone, and picked it up.

"Carruthers matched a fingerprint," Steve Ivey said excitedly.

"So soon?"

"We didn't have to bother Washington, Ed. We've got our boy on file right here in Tampa."

My hand curled hard on the phone. "At least that's a break."

"You said it! Ready for the run-down, Ed?"

"Ready." My throat grew slightly dry.

"His name is Ben McJunkin," Ivey said. "Ben as in the London clock. McJunkin as in——"

"I've got the name," I cut in. "Have you picked him up yet?"

"We've got a city-wide on him."

"Which should really rile him," I said. "Haven't you any good news?"

"It gets worse before it gets better," Ivey said dolefully. "He's a particularly mean one."

"Give it to me," I said.

"Straight out of our records, Ed." The lieutenant cleared his throat. "Ben McJunkin. Born March three, nineteen-two-one, Middlebury, Michigan. His father was a moderately successful grocer, comfortably middle class. As a youngster, Ben McJunkin was exposed to all the positive elements as recommended by child counselors and authorities. Good home. Security. Proper food and parental training. Not spoiled. Not deprived. In spite of it all, young Ben started getting in trouble before he was out of his teens.

"An older Ben played college football, was potentially a great star. They had to kick him off the squad for excessive brutality and keeping company with known gamblers and underworld characters. McJunkin dropped out of college in his junior year. He beat up, brutally, an assistant coach as a good-by gesture.

"Following his fling at college, Ben was in and out of a series of minor scrapes. Then he enlisted in the Marines in World War Two. He was one hell of a fighting man with a taste for carnage approaching the point of raw sadism. He capped off his military venture with a dishonorable discharge.

"In the ensuing years, Ben McJunkin has hardened into the pattern of the habitual and incorrigible criminal. He's run hot cars, wet-backed aliens across the Rio Grande, organized for a union of questionable legality, headed up a squad of hijackers. You name it, and it's in his record, including suspicion of robbery and murder. He was tried on these counts and acquitted for lack of evidence and refusal of witnesses to testify."

"Then he's never been nailed?" I asked.

"Oh, yes. Convicted and sentenced twice. Once on a charge of felonious assault, also for burglary."

"Then why the hell isn't he in the pokey where he belongs, Steve?"

"Parole boards. Twice paroled. Surprise you?"

"Like I would be surprised if the sun doesn't come up tomorrow," I said. "What's the local pitch?"

"He's been in and out of Tampa often," Steve said.

"Apparently he likes the winter climate and enjoys connections with underworld characters who drift south with the seasons. He ramrodded a bolita numbers racket here for a while. Nearly got polished off, too."

"What happened?"

"He got carved up," Steve said. "He was carried into an emergency room leaking blood in a dozen places. It was apparently the work of a colored sidekick with whom McJunkin had disagreed over the way the bolita take was cut. There wasn't enough evidence at the time to hold the Negro.

"A week after Ben McJunkin had convalesced, the colored yegg was found floating in Tampa Bay with a school of little fishes making lunch of his face."

"And not enough evidence there to hold McJunkin, I suppose," I said.

Steve was quietly miffed. "We have to go by the rules, Ed. You know that."

"Sure," I said. "Well, what do I look for?"

"Ben McJunkin's mug shot shows a big, good-looking guy," Steve said. "He's six feet, weights about two hundred, flat-bellied and solid. He's got a strong-boned, almost handsome face, hazel eyes, and dark-brown hair which is just beginning to thin. He has a thin white scar along his jawbone, right side, souvenir of his colored pal. He dresses well, like a substantial businessman of early middle age who has nothing to worry about. His personal habits are neat, orderly, clean. He likes women, doesn't booze to excess, and if he's ever made it with pot, we don't know it."

"I'll drop by for a copy of the mug shot," I said.

"It'll be waiting. Ed . . . I'd say that Ben McJunkin started in life with a sadistic streak that yearned for a thrill. But violence no longer holds excitement or a thrill for him. It has become a way of life.”

“Thanks for the warning, Steve.” I dropped the phone in its cradle slowly, without reassurance.

The couch creaked as Myrtle Higgins stirred. She looked at me with eyes heavy with a question, her face almost bovine. “The police, Ed?”

I nodded.

“Have they identified him?” she asked.

“A guy by the name of McJunkin.”

“Have they got him yet?”

“No,” I said, “and it’s not going to be like picking up a cocky young punk. This guy is a real pro with a thorough education—and I wish to hell I could put the members of a couple of parole boards in my shoes right now. . . .”

Myrtle swung her feet to the floor and sat thinking for several minutes. She reached for a cigarette, lighted it slowly, and brushed the dark-blond hair from her temples with her fingertips.

She looked at me carefully. “Well . . . too bad. Party’s over.” She stood up, sensuality fading from the lush lines of her body, and patted my cheek. “Call me a cab, Ed.”

“Tomorrow,” I said. “Not now, in the middle of the night.”

“Yes, now,” she said. “No more drink, no more fun, not tonight, Ed. This Ben McJunkin . . . he’s too big a shadow over this apartment right now.” She flicked my chin. “It’s deep, hard, and cold in your eyes, Ed, and I don’t like to look at them. So fetch me a cab, huh?”

“If you insist on going,” I said, “I’ll take you home.”

“Nuts. You don’t have to feel obligated. I’ll be okay.”

After she was gone, I stretched on the daybed and

stared in the darkness at the ceiling. By and by I was able to make out individual cracks. A dirty-looking gray light had stolen over the world outside. I punched my pillow, closed my eyes with resolve. And when I thought it was impossible, I drifted to sleep.

I was awake by eight o'clock, bathed, dressed and re-fueled with a breakfast of Cuban sausage, fried eggs, and black coffee the consistency of thin tar.

Most of the day was a slow-motion script taken from a routine report. I was here and there and all around in Ybor City, in the gin mills, the back rooms, the social clubs with Spanish names, the shops and stalls with their tourist-bait displays of alligator bags, beads, bangles, beaten-silver jewelry, guaraches.

I talked with characters in all shades from Nordic snow to African ebony. No longer faceless, his signature on my doorknob, the name of Ben McJunkin, assassin, became a web creeping across Ybor City. And Ybor City, I knew, saw the matter in that stark simplicity that is the height of all sophistication: The Moment of Truth approaches for Ed Rivers or Ben McJunkin. Which do we prefer in our midst?

Leaving the familiar, I drove to the rare feudal splendor of Señora Isabella's hacienda. Elena Sigmon responded to my knock. I wondered if she and her father were alone in the huge house, making do without servants.

Elena looked a bit older than her years today, showing the wear and tear of a long party. Clad in a sloppily loose T-shirt and tight shorts, her lean body sagged tiredly. A paleness lurked in her small pixie face. Her feathery, sun-bleached hair was carelessly combed. Her puffy eyes showed some irritation as she looked at me.

"Haven't they put you back under a rock yet?"

"There wasn't room," I said. "Couldn't squeeze me in. Your poah ole pappy here?"

She quirked a brow coolly at me, thought briefly. Then with the sinewy motion that reminded me of a lean little snake gliding across a warm stone, she turned and led the way into the expanses of the living room.

"Papa dear," she yelled, "the Cro-Magnon is on the loose again."

"Thanks," I said. "I'm trying hard to like you too."

"Don't strain yourself. There are too many things you wouldn't understand."

"Oh, I don't know. Sometimes you need only a few brush strokes to make a picture."

On her way toward a table where there were various breeds of liquor, she jerked to a stop. "I didn't know you were so interested in me."

"Deeply," I said.

"But the portrait, you know, depends on the artist and his interpretation, as much as on the subject."

"I haven't been talking to the wrong people," I said, "and I try to see below the tint to the right color."

"And who are these right people you've talked with?"

"Uh-uh," I said.

Her wide, expressive mouth twisted into a pout. "So keep your stinking little secrets and see if I care!"

She poured a drink, the neck of the bottle chattering against the glass. Without looking at me, she said, "Tell me about this picture you see."

"I'd rather not get personal."

"I insist," she said.

"Okay," I said. "You're part front."

"Only part?"

"We all have two faces. A public face—a secret face."

"And what do you think of my public face, Mr. Rivers?" She slid toward me, a drink in her hand, a spark of interest in her eyes.

"Spoiled. Self-centered. Vicious."

"And unprincipled?"

"Why not?" I asked.

"My! Do you also read palms? Let's get to my other face."

"Maybe it isn't clear, Elena—even to you."

The level of the liquid in her glass quivered. An old, hard wisdom came to her eyes. She turned suddenly and spoke toward the far wall: "You say one thing and mean the opposite, don't you?"

"If you'd admit what you see, maybe you wouldn't have to drink so much."

"Listen," she said thinly. "Nobody asked for your advice. I drink because I want to."

"Okay," I said.

"And I want to drink, drink, drink! I want to be pickled. I want to get drunk and stay that way."

"It wouldn't change the image of your father."

With her back still to me, she said, "I like the image. I like it fine."

"Sure. You enjoyed being alone in Caracas, receiving news that your grandmother Isabella had died in Tampa. It was just great, going up to a mountain cottage in that moment and finding your father there with Ginny Jameson."

Her shoulders stiffened. "You do get around, don't you? What do you know about Ginny Jameson?"

"I gather that she was a call girl operating in the upper

crust in Caracas, the latest on your father's little picnic when you walked in on them."

"You go to hell, Rivers!"

"It's too crowded. Too many people trying to get there."

"Meaning me, I suppose?"

"You'll have to answer that yourself," I said. "But there isn't enough booze in the world to drown certain kinds of memories."

"How would you know?"

Her question caused the brief eruption of memory of the dark, nightmarish years that had finally burned out in an Ybor City alley and on the docks of Port Tampa, where the labor was hard. "I read about it in a textbook," I said.

"It must have been a heavy one."

"It was. It says you inevitably reach a point where you got to do one of two things: die—or take hold of your bootstraps."

"Who wears boots, you nosy lug?"

"Try them on for size, Elena. You can't go back and keep the bomb from exploding. You can't reverse the clock or change the brain that conceived the bomb in Venezuela. Why don't you admit you're alone with your father, that the others are gone, your mother and grandfather when a timing device clicked inside a bomb, and finally your grandmother Isabella, who tried very hard to run away?"

The back of her shoulders made a small motion. She turned, and I saw that she was laughing.

"You think that's what bothers me?" she said, her voice rising with a cold, hard laugh. "You really think it? Man, you don't know from nothing!"

Eight

"What's going on?" Keith Sigmon said. He came across the room with plunging, angry strides. Emotion had pulled the dissipated edges of his face tight, restoring briefly his chiseled, classic good looks, in a cold, inhuman casting.

"This amateur psychiatrist," Elena said, "is trying to analyze me." She was pale. She looked at him with the laughter dying in her throat.

He gave her a quick but careful examination with his cutting gaze. Then he turned to me. "Rivers, do I have to put you under a peace bond to keep you away from here?"

"Nope."

"Don't you realize the police have upset us more than enough in the death of Jean Putnam?"

"Yep."

"Then what in hell are you after?"

"The continued existence of one Ed Rivers," I said, "for some years to come in a whole skin."

"Well . . ." he said. He thrust his hand in the pockets of his silk dressing gown. "I have no objection to your continued existence."

"Thanks."

"So long as you don't try to tear us to pieces in the process."

"He's trying," Elena said. Her tone was irritating,

egging Keith Sigmon. "He's torn his way back to Ginny Jameson."

Sigmon's lips thinned until they just about disappeared. "Go ahead and dig on that score, Rivers. The girl's death was an accident."

"Death?" I said. "I didn't know Ginny Jameson was dead."

I couldn't tell how my words reacted inside of Sigmon. This guy had lived by his wits and looks so many years it had become second nature. He shrugged. "Ginny and I had been partying a day or two in the cottage near Caracas. Elena came there with news of her grandmother Isabella's death in Tampa. Ginny decided the party was over, that father and daughter needs be alone at such a moment."

He motioned for Elena to get him a drink. "Ginny had been drinking. I tried to talk her out of driving back to Caracas alone. But . . . well, she and Elena had had words, rather bitter ones. And to be honest, I felt it time for Ginny to leave. Anyhow, she missed a turn on the mountain road. Elena and I spotted the wreckage when we left the cottage shortly afterward that night. I reported the accident to the authorities. The next day Elena and I came on to Tampa. That's all there was to it."

Nothing to him, I thought. Like a missing button on an old suit he's ready to cast off.

But it seemed likely that Elena didn't share his attitude and lack of feeling. I could imagine the scene in the mountain cottage when Elena had arrived that night. The news of her grandmother's death must have had her already in an emotional turmoil. To top it, to blow the lid off, she'd found herself crashing her father's liquor and sex party.

Later, recalling the things she'd said to her father and Ginny Jameson, perhaps Elena had felt responsible for sending the girl out to her accidental death.

Death on every hand for Elena Sigmon, little snake writhing on hot stone . . . Death by terrorist's bomb, death by age and decay in faraway Tampa, death by auto for a half-drunken girl on a mountain road at night.

For Elena, a more pleasant death lay in the bottle. Or so it appeared to me, right now, in this instant. How it would appear an hour from now, a day from now, I didn't know, because I didn't know what an hour from now might bring.

Sigmon accepted the drink his daughter offered. "Now that you've drawn me out on the subject of Ginny Jameson," he said, "I'm sure you'll excuse me. It's still Gasparilla time, you know. I have to dress for a cocktail party."

"It wasn't Ginny Jameson that brought me here," I said.

"Then what?"

"The old lady's brief case."

"Come again?" he said.

"Your mother-in-law, Señora Isabella Sorolla y Batione, deceased, owned an old leather portfolio. Jean Putnam reported it missing after the old lady died."

"So what?"

"Have you recovered it?"

"I don't think it's any of your business, Rivers."

"I do," I said. "It may be the right tag end."

"You're losing me on the curve again," he said.

"And I think it would be pretty hard to lose you on

any curve, any crooked twist. But I'll explain, Mr. Sigmon, Mr. Lord High Big Cheese of this palatial estate. Jean Putnam remained here for a few days after the old lady died to clear up tag ends. Somewhere in those tag ends was the one that caused Jean Putnam to want the services of a private detective. A tag end that got her killed."

"Ridiculous!"

"Want to tell me about that portfolio?"

"There's nothing to tell! It was simply an old catchall for an old woman's mementoes." He killed most of his drink at a gulp. "Try another tree, Rivers. You're barking up the wrong one here."

He stormed to the front door and held it open for me.

I flicked the door knocker with my finger. "Keep it polished."

"If you come back, you'd better have a good reason."

"I will," I said.

It was growing dark by the time I reached my apartment. I let the plumbing gargle, running the huge, old-fashioned tub almost to the brim. I stripped and soaked some of the mush out of my muscles in cool water.

I went out to dinner and got back about eight. I called police headquarters while I sipped a beer. Zero. Blank. The city-wide had failed as yet to net Ben McJunkin. I stood at the window while I finished the beer and thought of Ben McJunkin and the twists and turns his life had taken. It was hard to think of a scarred old panther like him as ever having been a chubby baby in a loving mother's arms.

Returning to the phone, I tried one or two numbers. Nobody was home. Everybody was out having a Gasparilla gas.

I watched my secondhand TV set for a while, one of the rare occasions when it was turned on, and there was snow in the picture.

The day had been endless. The previous night, with the varied experiences running the gamut from murderous McJunkin to merrymaking Myrtle, had taken a lot out of me. But my fatigue was due to something more than the physical. The apartment felt empty, as if no one at all lived here. A yawning emptiness seemed to be at my feet.

I made sure the windows and doors were locked. I turned in early. I slept with the .38 near my right hand.

When I reached my office the next morning, the telephone-answering service reported a call from Fred Eppling, the attorney. He'd left a number for me to call back. I called, and he answered the phone himself. He said he wanted to see me and gave me an address in a staid bank building a few blocks away.

I walked over. Eppling's suite of offices was on the second floor, quietly sumptuous, a layout of satin-sheened walnut paneling, leather furniture, draperies of raw silk, and diffused indirect lighting.

His neat, smallish, sandy presence was clad in a three-hundred-dollar suit as if it was his work clothes—which it was.

His slightly sallow face had a few lines of strain. He smiled vaguely. "Seems we have another thing in common, Rivers—both working on a Gasparilla play-day."

"The costumed *señoritas* in Ybor City will just have to get along without us."

He glanced at his wrist watch. "I'm due at police headquarters at eleven o'clock to go over some details relating to Señora Isabella's estate."

"Anything to do with Jean Putnam's death?"

"Who can say? Frightening . . . If a girl like Jean is subject to murder, none of us is safe."

"I get the same sentiment on every hand," I said. "But the least likely victim is nevertheless stone-cold dead in the morgue."

He nodded, almost casually. He was making no display. Neither does a man who feels a thing deep down, where it will stay with him a long time . . .

"Any men in her life?" I suggested.

"Jean's? Wrong street, Rivers. Several young men, all of good character. But no deep entanglements. No wild-eyed rejected suitor who'd hire a professional killer."

"You never know what goes on behind a man's eyes."

The corner of Eppling's mouth quirked. He made a gesture encompassing the office. "It wasn't always like this, Rivers. I worked my way through law school and started from scratch in criminal law. I took any cases I could get, working and driving for opportunity. I haven't always been the sheltered corporation lawyer. I know what the human brain can harbor."

"Then we come back to Señora Isabella," I said. "An old woman dies of natural causes, nothing shady, nothing haywire. But a girl apparently as noble as Joan of Arc is subsequently marked for murder. Something Jean did for the old Señora?"

"Impossible! Jean's duties were wholly innocent. She screened the continual charity seekers, oversaw household expenditures, made out checks for the old lady's personal charge accounts, handled personal correspondence, kept the *señora*'s social appointment book straight. That sort of thing."

His voice shaded off. He was in a funk for a second. "Those were pleasant days for Jean Putnam, Rivers. Gracious living, genteel environment. The old lady was really fond of her."

"Maybe Jean Putnam filled a gap left by a dead daughter."

"No," Eppling said slowly. "It wasn't that, at least not bascially. The *señora* was tough, the way a queen could be tough when monarchies were for real. She was hard to get close to. She talked little of the past. She had plenty of emotional control. She was kind and patient, but she didn't go in for deep friendships. And she permitted herself to despise only two things in life—Venezuelan terrorists and her rotten son-in-law."

Nine

With a conscious effort, Eppling snapped the morbid train of thought. An attitude of briskness returned to his body. "I had several reasons for wanting to see you," he said. "Shall we get started on them?"

"Fine."

"The first has to do with Señora Isabella's will," Eppling said. "To lead up to Jean Putnam, I suppose I should acquaint you with the old lady's wishes in general terms.

"She had two heirs apparent, her granddaughter Elena

and the despised son-in-law, Keith Sigmon. Frankly, the old woman was happy with neither prospect. But she was dead set against Keith Sigmon ever coming into control of the estate.

"Cutting through the legalistic language and complicated technicalities, the old lady earmarked the bulk of the estate to Elena, thence eventually upon Elena's demise to several charities and foundations.

"Now in an estate of such awesome proportions, a few thousand here and there is chicken feed. This is where Jean Putnam fits in. The old *señora* left little bequests to everyone around her, including the grocery delivery man. The largest went to Jean Putnam, ten thousand dollars in cash. She didn't live to spend a penny of it. Somewhere, Jean must have a blood relation, if simply a distant cousin. This person, or persons, is now her heir. I want your assistance in finding him, her, or them."

"I'll have to file it for future attention," I said.

"I know," he nodded, "but there is the chance you'll run across the information in your present investigation. If not, get to it as quickly as you can. I naturally want the will probated and the estate settled as soon as possible."

He glanced past me suddenly in a way that caused me to swivel my head. The office door had opened silently on oiled hinges. Van Clavery stood in the doorway, his eyes baleful in his lean, anxiety-ridden face.

Eppling touched my arm briefly. "My second reason for calling you, Rivers." He took a few steps across the office. "Come in, Van," he said quietly, "and close the door."

Clavery obeyed, his movements jerky with irritation

or something deeper. He wore a dark business suit, but I still got that impression of uncertainty of Clavery's re-actions, that sense of danger that he'd somehow conveyed in the pirate costume when I'd first met him.

Clavery and the lawyer exchanged a brief message with their eyes. The silence of the office became notice-able.

"I'm glad you came, Van," Eppling said quietly.

Clavery's lips thinned. "I hope I'm not making a mistake."

"I gave you the best advice I could, Van."

"Or put a rope around my neck!"

"I don't think so," Eppling said. "I know Rivers by reputation. He'll dredge up every detail, if he lives so long. It won't look good if he finds it out for himself. As I told you on the phone, it's better to give it to him, straight out, now."

Clavery looked at me with eyes that for a fractured second hated me unreasonably, hated me as a symbol of something he'd like to smash.

Eppling said, "Van has a few words of a personal nature he'd like to say, Rivers. Will you offer your professional confidence?"

"Tentatively," I said.

"Then to hell with it!" Clavery said, as if he were at a breaking point.

Eppling put his hand on Clavery's shoulder. "Now wait a minute, Van. Rivers is in a touchy position him-self. If what you have to say was against Rivers' interests, we wouldn't consider it, wouldn't be here. If it isn't against his interests, I'm sure he will treat it with confi-dence."

"I'm not known as a talebearer," I said.

Clavery moved a few steps, aimlessly, just for the sake of moving.

"Well, Van?" Eppling prompted.

Clavery fingered his lips as if trying to bring feeling back to them. "Several months ago . . . I spotted a stock deal that looked sure-fire. I . . . borrowed money to make the play."

"From the *señora's* timber-import enterprise?" I asked.

"Yes . . ." His voice was the rattle of paper. His admission had killed the anger in him, taken a part of the life out of him. "The deal fell through. I was caught short."

"How much?"

"Forty thousand dollars," he said. A short, irrational laugh ripped from him. "Didn't seem like much at the time, stacked against the prospects . . . but it's all the money in the world if you haven't got it."

He looked at me as if he had to focus his eyes all over again. "Recently . . . when I knew an accounting was bound to reveal the shortage . . . I went to Señora Isabella, told her what had happened, and asked for a little time."

"You couldn't raise the money?"

"I'd raised every dime I could, to go with the forty thousand. Even my home . . . isn't worth the paper against it." Clavery stumbled to a chair and dropped. He sat grasping the chair arms, a quivering in his hunched body.

"I was counting on my past record, the old lady's gentility and common sense," he said. "Throwing me in jail wouldn't get her money back."

"She went along?"

Clavery looked at me bleakly. "She was deeply hurt.

I hated myself for doing that to her. She thought it over for a few days. Then she called me, the week before she died. I hurried to see her . . ."

He shook his head against the overpowering clutch of his personal ghosts. "The old lady was looking better, feeling better, able to sit near her bedroom window. The last upsurge before death, I guess it was. She greeted me normally, as if it was a routine business discussion. Said she'd decided how the matter should be handled. She wanted my personal note in amount of forty thousand dollars, payable in five equal annual installments. She also wanted a brief statement in my own handwriting as to the indebtedness covered by the note. Naturally I gave her both."

"Naturally."

"She clipped the note and statement together and put them in a large old leather portfolio," Clavery said. "She assured me the matter would forever remain between the two of us."

I glanced at Eppling. "When did you learn about this?"

"At the start. Señora Isabella asked my advice before making a decision. I saw no profit in destroying Van for a single mistake."

"A couple days after the old lady died," Clavery said, "Fred and I went to the hacienda. He'd agreed to separate my . . ." his face twisted, "my confession and the five-year note. The statement was to go here in the office safe."

Eppling regarded me coolly. "The indebtedness had to be included in the assets of the estate," he said. "But Van's personal statement had no business going to a probate judge, as I saw it. He and Señora Isabella had settled the matter between them. I was handling it as she would have wished. The handwritten statement, which Van terms a confession, was to be returned to him when he had repaid the forty thousand."

Clavery worked his hands together, popping the knuckles like brittle sticks. "Jean Putnam went to get the portfolio for Fred——"

"And discovered it was missing," I said.

They both drilled me with their attention.

"Where'd you learn that?" Clavery said.

"You don't expect me to answer that, do you?" I countered. "I suppose you searched for the brief case."

"Thoroughly," Fred Eppling said.

Clavery began to gasp. "I intend to repay the money, even if the confession is never found . . . but that statement . . . in my own handwriting . . . made public, it would brand me, shatter my reputation, ruin my life . . ."

A sudden seizure stiffened Clavery's wiry body. His tongue curled in a wad toward his throat. His eyes rolled upward until the whites showed. He grabbed his chest.

"Get some water," I told Eppling.

I slid Clavery from the chair and stretched his rigid body on the plush carpet. I heard Eppling rattling glassware in the next office.

By the time I'd loosened Clavery's collar and straightened his arms at his sides, Eppling had returned with the glass in his hand.

"Brandy," Eppling. "Better than water."

Clavery's body was relaxing in a series of shudders. I slipped my hand behind his head, lifted slightly, and put the brandy to his lips. The amber liquid rolled into his mouth, a few drops at a time. I sensed strength returning to his muscles.

My face became distinct in his burning-eyed gaze. He pushed at me weakly, slowly sat up. "Fred . . ."

"Yes?" Eppling said from across the room.

"What are you doing?"

"Phoning for a doctor." Eppling, I saw, was standing with a phone in his hand.

"Never mind," Clavery said. "I'm all right now."

"But, Van . . ."

"For God's sake, don't weary me!" Clavery shouted weakly. "Do as I say and put the phone down!"

"It may be your heart, Van."

"No such luck," Clavery said through twisted lips. He struggled into the chair with my help. "I've had all that checked. A nervous syndrome. The medics have a name for it, but it's plain damned stinking nerves . . ."

His eyes filled with self-hatred and a wild frustration. "This." He pummeled his thighs, belly, and chest. "This isn't me, this wad of corruption, this mass of flesh and blood and bone. The part that thinks and feels . . . that's me. That's the personality, the entity known as Van Clavery! But it—the *me*—is imprisoned in this faulty vessel, this morass, this barbed-wire, inescapable jail of lousy nerves."

His breath was thinning again. I wondered if he was on the verge of another spasm.

He peered at me with eyes that had redness in their rims. His nostrils flared. "Damn you," he said bitterly. "Big, solid man . . . no quakes . . . no shivers . . . you don't *know*. You can't understand. So don't stand there and pity me! I—the *me*—can't stand your stupid pity."

Clavery dropped his haggard face in his hands. A thin,

mewling sound came from him. It was a sob, deep and bitter inside of him and unable to find its way clearly out of him.

Over Clavery's head, my gaze met that of Eppling. We stared at each other a moment, slightly shamed and fearful with the reminder between us of the capacities and incapacities inherent in all men.

Eppling's eyes fell away. He studied the top of his friend's head for a moment, standing behind the chair.

"Rivers . . . if you get a lead on the portfolio, will you call me? It will be worth one thousand dollars if you call me."

"What was in the brief case?" I said.

"I'm not sure," Eppling said. "I never examined it. The *señora* used it as a depository for personal odds and ends. I imagine it was junk, except for the personal meaning it had for her. And, of course, excepting Van's five-year note and handwritten statement."

"The statement might give someone wrong ideas," I suggested. "Has there been any contact, any hint at blackmail?"

"Not that I know of," Eppling said. "Has there, Van?"

Clavery didn't immediately answer. Eppling touched his shoulder. "Did you understand me, Van?"

"Yes," Clavery said, jerking away. "I understand. I've got nerves, but I'm not a frigging mental case!"

He lunged out of the chair, burning up his reserves. He strode to the window and stood looking out. When he turned, he was calmer.

"Sorry, Fred."

"Forget it. You're under one hell of a strain."

Clavery nodded absently, as if for the moment he was beyond caring. "Fat chance anybody would have of blackmailing me, Rivers. I halfway wish something like that would happen. It would at least break the uncertainty, the blank. It would give me a chance to get that confession back—even if I had to kill the bastard who took it."

"If anybody makes contact," I said, "you contact me."

"Maybe I don't——"

"You contact me," I repeated. "My neck is involved, and the disappearance of the old lady's portfolio is the only break I've got so far. You follow?"

Clavery looked at me in morbid silence, but I knew he got the message.

Ten

Back in my office, I put an overseas phone call to Caracas, Venezuela, on the agency bill. The member of the Caracas *policía* who put me on his switchboard spoke badly fractured English. My Spanish was little better. He got the drift of what I was after finally and connected me with a higher-up who spoke better English than I did.

Carrying an honorary membership card in the Florida Sheriff's Association and being on the rolls of the Tampa auxiliary police force, I stretched a point and told the *capitán* in Caracas that I was a Tampa cop.

"What may we do for you, Señor Rivers?"

"We are investigating a murder," I said. "The victim

was one Jean Putnam, formerly employed by the Señora Isabella Sorolla y Batione."

"Ah, yes. A fine old lady. We were sorry to hear of her death."

"We are interested in her son-in-law, Keith Sigmon," I said.

"I'm acquainted with the name only through the investigation of the bombing that took the life of his wife and father-in-law."

"Was he clean on that score?"

"Señor! You suspect . . . but no! The bombing was most definitely the work of terrorists. Keith Sigmon has a vile reputation, but he has taken care not to fall into our official records."

"He was not in Caracas when word was received there of the old *señora*'s death," I said. "He was at a mountain cottage with a girl named Ginny Jameson. The girl was killed while driving from the cottage toward Caracas."

"One moment, please. I will have to consult the record."

The phone company rang up a little more profit while the *capitán* barked orders in Spanish and apologized to me for the brief delay.

I heard him murmur, *"Gracias, Luis,"* heard the rustle of paper. Then: "I have it, Señor Rivers. The matter was mainly handled by the constabulary of the mountain village of Eminencia. We entered the investigation at Keith Sigmon's request."

"His request?"

"He was anxious to make his departure for Tampa, in view of the death of his mother-in-law. The accident, while unfortunate, had no suspicious aspects.The girl, Ginny Jameson, was a known prostitute. She came to

Caracas from the United States with a company of entertainers. When the others returned, Ginny Jameson remained. As a dancer she had little talent, but she found other employment pleasurable and reasonably profitable. Had she lived, I'm sure we would have eventually deported her."

"But she saved you the trouble," I said.

"Well . . . since you put it that way."

"Keith Sigmon says she left the mountain cottage alone," I said.

"We are certain of it. No one could have been in the car with her and escaped serious injury. The vehicle overturned on her, pinning her inside, and caught fire. That stretch of road is desolate, Señor Rivers. Had it not been for the flames, she might have lain undiscovered in the ravine for days. As it was, Sigmon saw the wreckage and reported it immediately . . . . not the action of a man who is hiding anything, I might reflect. He might have conveniently had a lapse of memory and boarded his plane the next day."

"Then his skirts are clean," I said.

"On that score, absolutely. Our experts examined the scene, the wreckage. Ginny Jameson was driving at a high rate of speed, as the skid marks showed. She simply went off the sharp curve to her death. We—how do you put it in your idiom?—shoveled up the remains of her and interred her without mourners. At the state's expense, I might add."

"At least you were rid of her."

"Be it so," he said. "We welcome Americans almost without exception. This one was an exception."

"As well as Keith Sigmon."

"Well, we do hope he remains with you. A questionable man—but in the matter of Ginny Jameson the evidence made Keith Sigmon's word indisputable."

I thanked him and hung up the phone. I sat cracking brain cells for a few minutes. Then I got up and started to leave the office, but I didn't. Natalie Clavery was coming in.

In a crisp linen suit, she looked as cool and endurable as polished marble. Her eyes were clear, slightly aloof. Her black hair was a glistening frame for the perfection of her face.

Without preamble, she said, "Was confession good for my husband's soul, Mr. Rivers?"

"Probably."

"Then he did talk to you?"

"Yes, if you're referring to forty thousand dollars that stuck to his fingers," I said.

"That's one way of putting it. I hope the information isn't in the wrong hands."

"Tit for tat," I said. "Look, why don't we start over? Have a chair, call me Ed, and we'll try to bridge this gulf our instincts has built between us."

She thought about it. The shield of haughtiness slipped slightly from her eyes. "Which chair may I take, Ed?"

I got out a handkerchief, dusted off a chair, and she smiled at the gesture. "If Señora Isabella had lived, my husband was legally clear—provided he made the payments stipulated by his promissory note. The old lady had refused to press charges, and the matter was settled."

"So I've been told," I said.

"Now, however, if Elena Sigmon has the note and that very incriminating statement in Van's handwriting, she's in a position to do more than make mere trouble."

"What makes you think Elena——"

"Who else, Ed? When Fred Eppling told Elena that her grandmother's old portfolio was missing, Elena passed it off lightly. Quite casually she said the brief case would probably turn up."

I gave Natalie Clavery an intent look. "You don't like Elena at all."

"Frankly, I have an instinctive abhorrence of her. We were all strangers here. We expected a bereaved girl. Instead, we were treated to a misbegotten brat!"

"Strong words."

"Wait until you've known Elena better," Natalie Clavery said. "I think her father's influence has destroyed any good qualities that might have been in Elena. At any rate I've got to get that handwritten statement of Van's back." She looked at me obliquely. "Do you know what it will do to a man of my husband's temperament to be publicly branded a thief?"

I remembered the way Clavery's nerve-wracked body had twitched on the carpeting in Fred Eppling's office. "I've an idea."

"He would kill himself," she said simply. The polished surface didn't crack, but I glimpsed the things that lived in her eyes. My very first impression of her returned stronger than ever. Underneath the gloss there was plenty of woman. The man to whom she gave herself would never need or even want another woman.

"Van Clavery, in one respect at least, is a very lucky man," I said.

"Thank you," she said simply. "He happens to be my husband."

"If he filched that portfolio himself," I pointed out, "it would save him forty thousand dollars, not to mention the pleasure of destroying a statement of guilt."

"And I'm not above wishing he had done so," she said candidly.

"He could then have rung in Fred Eppling to throw suspicion from himself."

"But he didn't, Ed."

"Would you tell me if he had?"

"No," she said. "But I'd have no reason for being here right now if he had."

"Maybe he glommed onto the brief case and didn't tell you."

She shook her head, gave me a patient look. "He would have told me. He knows he can trust me. He would have been considerate, sparing me unnecessary worry and anxiety. No, you know the truth of it—the brief case has fallen into unknown hands."

"And Jean Putnam knew whose hands?"

"Isn't it possible?" she asked. "People have been killed for less value than a promissory note in amount of forty thousand dollars, not to mention evidence of embezzlement that someone might regard as of equal value."

"If I happen to turn up the brief case, do you want me to bring it to you?"

"Oh, no," she said with a motion of her hand. "Deliver it to Fred Eppling. Van made one mistake, Ed. The single mistake he's made in his life. Later he faced it, squared it. We want the old *señora*'s wishes carried out, that's all."

"Since you put it that way," I said, "I'll do my best for you."

"We will pay a reasonable fee, of course."

"I'll charge you one, of course."

A faint laugh came from her. "I feel a little better now. You—big, ruffian-looking man that you are . . .

You have revised my first impression of you. You are a paradox."

"Most of us are. Just two-legged bundles of contrasts."

She rose gracefully and moved toward the door. She paused and said casually, "Van didn't want me to see you, but I had to satisfy myself. Now I'm glad. I'm also glad I don't have to fight you, Ed. For Van I should fight in any way, with any means at my disposal."

"Okay," I said, "and I'm one of the means."

"I hadn't quite thought of it that way. Do you resent it?"

"A little," I said honestly. "But I haven't been given many choices since Jean Putnam picked up a phone and called my number."

When Natalie Clavery was gone, I ankled over to police headquarters. They didn't know a damn thing I didn't know. They'd picked up no trace of Ben McJunkin, and I had a moment filled with the illogical premonition that they never would.

They'd talked with Jean Putnam's roommate, Lura Thackery, getting no more from her than I had. Jean Putnam's nearest and dearest friend was certainly keeping her skirts clean.

Back in the office, I picked up the phone and draped a handkerchief over the mouthpiece.

I hesitated. Then I reached forward and dialed Lura Thackery's number, and the swing of the dial reminded me of a screw tightening.

Eleven

Her polished little voice said, "Hello?"

I didn't speak right away, letting her listen to the emptiness of the open phone line. Her voice went up a notch: "Hello? . . . Who is calling, please?"

I frown on certain language in the presence of a lady; but I had to remember that McJunkin, or whoever was behind him, would not have been civilized with Lura Thackery. They'd have left no doubts in her as to her position and their intentions.

As McJunkin might have done, I let out a heavy breath and said softly, "You cruddy, big-mouthed bitch."

The alien idiom caused her to shrink in silence. My pulse rate picked up a beat. Her failure to question the reason for the call or demand the identity of the speaker meant that she believed she knew who was calling and why. My first hunch about Lura Thackery had been correct.

"You were warned to stay away from Ed Rivers," I said.

"I didn't go to him," she said in a voice edged with panic.

"You talked to him."

"He came to me. You've got to believe me!"

"Rivers isn't telling it that way," I said.

"Then he's lying. He's trying to fool you. I gave you the diary, didn't I? I promised to mind my own business."

Diary?

I pulled erect in my office chair. Whose diary? Jean Putnam's?

"Why do you keep hounding me?" Lura was saying. "Why don't you leave me alone?"

"You're in it whether you like it or not," I said through the handkerchief.

"I don't want to be in it!" Her voice had gone shrill.

"That's tough. Rivers is the one who might make the kind of trouble I don't like. The cops, they got rules. They'll handle you with kid gloves. Rivers makes his own rules sometimes."

"You're scared of Rivers!" she cried.

"Listen, you crummy slut——"

"And you hate me . . . I know it . . . Everyone hates me. My mother. My father. Even the psychiatrist." She was nearing hysteria. "You're looking for an excuse to make me like Jean. Why should I do anything more for you?"

"Because I say so, creep. You got to take your pick. Me or Ed Rivers."

I slipped the handkerchief from the phone and quietly hung up.

Unhappily, I sat. I hadn't liked doing it. I was sorry for the misty-eyed girl with the transluscent skin who had walked too closely to the dark edges of life.

I waited, giving her time. Ten minutes. Twenty.

I began to frown at the phone. Then it rang. I let it ring a second time before I picked it up.

"Nationwide Detective Agency," I said. "Ed Rivers speaking."

"This is Lura Thackery." Her voice was unsteady, with intermittent snubbing sounds, the aftermath of hard sobbing.

"I'm glad to hear from you," I said.

"Are you?" she said remotely. "You've got me in trouble, you know."

"Have I?"

"Talking about Jean's diary. Going around trying to find it. Who told you about it?"

"Why the interest, Miss Thackery? I though you were going to keep yourself nice and clean, like a cutely starched little girl."

"You beast," she sobbed. "You jungle animal!"

"Want to tell me about the diary?"

"I want to live," she pleaded. "I don't want . . . what happened to Jean. I want you to stop making an effort to get me killed."

"I didn't hold the gun that put the bullet in Jean Putnam's back," I reminded her. "Therein lies your danger—not from me."

"You!" She sobbed, her voice thick with raw bitterness. "If Jean hadn't been going to see you, none of this would have happened."

"Why not accept what's happened," I suggested, "and go on from there?"

"Go on to what? You weren't able to keep Jean alive!"

"I didn't have the chance. I might have with you."

She broke into uncontrolled weeping. Mingled with her sobs were ragged words. "I wish you didn't exist . . . had never been born . . . I wish you were dead!"

"Miss Thackery, if I accommodated everybody who's wished that, I'd need the total lives of half a dozen cats. The fact is, I continue. I intend to continue long after the man who has threatened you is gone."

"Words . . . empty words . . . how many stupid words

have been given me in the face of cold reality . . . words for as long as I can remember."

"The cold reality of Ben McJunkin won't go away because you wish it, Miss Thackery. But words might help—your words."

"You're trying to confuse me," she said, weeping, "because you hate me."

She was cowering behind defenses she'd built out of neurotic material. Trying to get through to her was like attempting to cut a shadow with a knife.

"I know how the image of McJunkin must appear to you," I said patiently, "grotesque and evil and all-powerful. The image is the more terrifying because it comes at you from a world outside your knowledge and experience."

"You can't know how I *feel*." She sobbed.

"Maybe I can," I soothed. "I'm trying very hard."

"I have the evidence of what he did to Jean," she said, "and all you can give me is words. It doesn't matter to him what he does now."

I remembered words McJunkin had spoken against my ear, with a gun against my back. "You mean the murder of one person is like taking out a license to murder many?"

"Yes . . . he . . . almost the words he said to me."

At least, I had one thing at this point. There was no remaining shred of doubt now that it was Ben McJunkin who had terrorized her.

"Then you must surely realize, Miss Thackery, that he's got to be stopped. For your own sake. Because he feels he has a license to kill." I gave her a second to think about it. "You are living because he extends to you the privilege. With a man like McJunkin how do you know when or on what whim he will decide to revoke the privilege?"

"I won't listen! You enjoy being cruel to me!"

My lips pulled flat against my teeth. Okay, I thought, if I can't appeal to your courage, Miss Thackery, we'll try a play on your cowardice.

"Get this, stupid," I said coldly, "I don't enjoy being anything to you, because you're a nothing. Living by permission of a punk is all you deserve. Jean Putnam, the friend you've turned your back on, had more worth in her little finger than you've got in your whole being. You've convinced me I shouldn't give a damn what happens to you. That's the way you want it, that's the way you'll get it."

"What are you saying to me?" she cried.

"I'm sick of you. I'm through with you. The hell with you. McJunkin can't afford to let you live indefinitely. If you're too dumb to see that, I couldn't care less. So long, Miss Thackery——and happy dying."

"Wait!" she screamed softly. "Don't hang up . . . Please don't hang up."

"I don't think we have any more to say. I wanted to help you in order to help myself. You ought to be able to see that. But it's a two-way street. And I don't need your help nearly as much as you need mine. You'll sit and wait to die because you've cut yourself off from help. But I've got ways and means. I've taken care of myself so far. I can continue to do so. I'll get to Ben McJunkin eventually. You'd better hope I do before he ends your waiting. He might take more time with you than he did with Jean Putnam. You never know. He might decide to tear your clothes off and have some fun before he puts the period on your life sentence."

"I can't stand any more of this! I can't . . . I can't!"

"Then put a stop to it."

She broke into a fresh fit of weeping. It wasn't just a woman crying. It was the expression of an animal in raw torment. I wanted to drop the phone from my ear to get away from the sound.

"Let me think . . ." She sobbed. "Give me some time . . . come to see me . . . at six o'clock."

"I'll be there, Miss Thackery."

Cradling the phone, I got up and crossed the office to get a drink of water. There was little joy in my brief and partial triumph over Lura Thackery. I felt as if I'd been touched by something alien, like brushing into a sticky cobweb in the darkness.

At five-fifty-five that afternoon, while Tampa readied for another gala Gasparilla evening, I parked in front of the apartment building on Calmwaters Boulevard.

The door was open at the first apartment I passed. The noise of gay people and bright music spilled into the corridor as a cocktail party got off the ground.

The sliding door of the self-service elevator separated me from all the happy people. The wooden-paneled box with the thick carpeting purred me up to the second floor. The door sighed open, and I walked the short distance to the Thackery-Putnam apartment.

I laid my thumb against the buzzer, waited, and tried again.

By the fourth buzz, my blood pressure had risen a notch. I hadn't broken down her ingrained habit of flight, of never facing anything, after all. I wondered how much distance she'd been able to put between herself and Tampa during the afternoon. Trying to run far enough from a thing like murder was hardly a rational act; but then, she was hardly a rational girl.

I glanced the length of the corridor. It was very quiet. I slipped my key ring from my pocket and separated the thin steel from the keys.

I didn't need the steel. When I tried the knob, it turned. The door was unlocked.

I slipped inside the apartment and stood a moment, listening. With Lura Thackery, odd possibilities became probabilities. I wondered fleetingly if the snarl of the door buzzer had brought an upsurge of fear and uncertainty in her, causing her to cower motionless in the apartment.

I checked out the possibility by moving from the door and taking a quick glance through the apartment, including the outside balcony with its furnishings of glass and wrought iron.

My first guess started to hold water again. She'd apparently flaked out.

The back of my neck warmed from frustration, disappointment. I needed Lura Thackery almost as much as she needed me. I doubted that she would have had the temerity to read another person's diary, but she could vouch for the fact that one had existed with Jean Putnam's personal report of what she had seen and heard during her last days on earth.

If there had been a diary, there might have been other things. A letter. A jotted note or phone number. A name in an address book.

I started with the desk and bookcases. The most I got was an idea of their diet from an old grocery order Jean or Lura had written and an acquaintance with the kind of books they'd read.

I moved into the bedroom, where the far wall was a circular arch of windows and the furnishings were as feminine and dainty as lace. The nightstands and dressing tables yielded a partly empty package of cigarettes, a few soft-cover books for end-of-the-evening relaxation, and a generous supply of cosmetics that looked expensive.

The closet door slid silently open under my touch.

My first guess spilled all its water instantly. Lura Thackery hadn't run away.

She was crouched on the floor of the closet. With the removal of the supporting closet door, her thin form began to move. She rolled to one side, slowly at first like a streamer of delicate cloth floating downward. With a soft bumping of her shoulder, she came to rest half in and half out of the closet.

I dropped to one knee, touched her face, turned her head slightly.

Her neck was swollen almost out to her chin. Across the swelling lay a deep crease. The crease ran around her neck, all the way to the nape.

That's where the ends of the loop of wire stuck out.

Twelve

"I know how you feel, Ed, but you can't possibly blame yourself." Homicide Lieutenant Steve Ivey was speaking while the tech men went about their grim job in Lura Thackery's apartment.

"Who said anything about blame?" I asked.

"Nobody—but it's in your face."

"I was thinking," I said, "of the little actions in life and the way they always spread out. Specifically, of McJunkin's visit to my apartment and of my knife throw. This, today, might have never happened, if the throw had been a few inches different."

"You did pretty well, Ed, considering the circumstances."

"I thought I had hurt him. He went out of my building with the blade in him."

"And he's tough," Ivey said. "We've checked every doctor in town. None has treated a knife wound in a man answering McJunkin's description. He carried the knife away, and he pulled it out, and he plugged up the hole. It didn't slow him down, Ed—not enough."

Steve watched two ambulance men cross the room with Lura Thackery's sheet-covered body on a stretcher between them.

"Death of the innocents," Steve muttered. "Two girls who never hurt anybody, except themselves. Jean Putnam didn't want to bring a suspicion into the open without having a private detective confirm it. Killed by her own sense of consideration for her fellow man, you might say. Lura Thackery—killed by her fear."

Between the meat-wagon boys Lura Thackery went through the doorway, out of the apartment for the last time.

Ivey watched the stretcher until it was out of sight in the corridor. "Maybe her fear was too much bigger than her belief that you could help her, Ed. Maybe she got to thinking, after she called you, and made the wrong decision. Maybe she contacted McJunkin, begged him to leave her alone, and tipped him that the pressure was on her."

"Could be," I said.

"Or maybe," Steve shrugged, "McJunkin simply found the opportunity today to carry out the intention that must have been in his mind from the start. Either way, Lura Thackery wrote the first line of her own obituary when she handed Jean Putnam's diary over to McJunkin. She became a sheep marked for slaughter."

Ivey took a final look around the tasteful little apartment. "From the prelim work here," he said, "we've a good idea of how McJunkin did it. He probably came exuding friendliness and reassurance until he'd lulled the girl's worst fears. Inside the apartment, when she least expected it, he clipped Lura Thackery on the chin—which accounts for the bruise the coroner found. While she was unconscious, McJunkin methodically helped himself to a wire coat hanger, wrapped it around her neck, twisted it tight. He stuffed her in the closet and left as quiet as he had come."

"Now you hit the jackpot question," I said.

"I know," Ivey said grayly. "Where did he leave to? What was his destination?"

I kept trying to pull a mental lever on the jackpot as I drove toward Ybor City. I was bugged with a sense of frustration, a feeling that something, somewhere along the line, had escaped my conscious notice.

I crept into Ybor City, moving with the massed Gasparilla crowds and traffic.

In the heart of the Quarter, sidewalk stalls had been set up, gaily decorated. At these stalls *señoritas* in flowing skirts, drawstring blouses, and lace mantillas were ladling out bowls of free garbanzo soup. Swarms of *turistas* lapped up the soup and ogled the *señoritas*.

I was reminded of the fact of hunger. I stopped at a Spanish restaurant and stoked the engine with the first-rate fuel of crawfish *sarapico*. A balmy evening was stretching over the Gulf when I returned to the car, got in, and aimed it in the direction of the Señora Isabella hacienda.

The deceased *doña*'s castle was brilliant with light when I arrived. Many of the downstairs windows glittered, and paper lanterns had been strung over the courtyard.

At the outer edge of the courtyard two large outdoor grills had been set up. A suckling pig and chickens were turning on spits, attended by a fat chef. A willowy babe in a scanty excuse for a maid's uniform was arranging glasses on a table that would serve for a bar near the fountain. In powder-blue dinner jacket and horn-rimmed glasses, a young man with a musical-instrument case in his hand had paused to gas with the barmaid.

She was laughing at something he'd said when I walked up. She gave me a cool glance, and the musician, lounging against the table, gave me a languid one.

"You delivering something for the party?" the girl asked.

"Nope. Mr. Sigmon or his daughter around?"

"I don't believe they've come back yet. Just us people from the catering service."

"And the combo leader." The musician yawned.

"I'll wait," I said.

There was traffic in and out of the house as the

caterers made ready for the festivities. The musician ambled along as I went inside.

As we descended to the acreage of the living room, he lighted a cigarette with a suspicious smell. "Dig this pad, Pops!"

"It's twenty-three skiddoo, son," I said.

He laughed, gave me a second look. "Cool, Pops. Say, aren't we acquainted?"

"I don't think so."

"I've seen you around. Ybor City. Or in the papers. Or," he snickered, "with a face like that, in here." He explained where "in here" was by waggling his cigarette.

His attention drifted. He was looking the room over.

"They'll plant us there, by the piano, I guess. Acoustics lousy. But who makes with acoustic trouble, playing for a babe come into all her green? Tell me, Pops, is this Elena Sigmon married?"

"Why don't you ask her yourself?"

"You're with it, man! Sure, why not?"

He drifted rather limply toward the piano. He dismissed me from his area of existence the second his back was toward me. The action was mutual. I'd dismissed him from mine by the time I went quietly from the room.

I was in a corridor with parquet flooring and an arched overhead. As the long porticoes facing the courtyard provided an outdoorsy connection between the three wings of the U-shaped house, I suspected that this hallway was an inside link from the living room to the adjacent wing.

The first door I passed was a stout oaken portal with a small crucifix attached at head height. I stopped, turned back, remembering that one word—"incense"—which Jean Putnam had spoken as she died.

I opened the door and gazed at the small private chapel where old Señora Isabella Sorolla y Batione had bent her aged kness and paid homage to her God.

If Jean Putnam had been trying to direct me to the chapel, I had no idea why. The place was barren, almost cold feeling now. No candles burned. The air was stale. I was of the opinion that the chapel hadn't been opened since the old lady had died.

I closed the door, turned, and moved on. The hallway right-angled, paralleling the outside portico. I could look through the windows, under the portico arches, and see the preparations for the festivities going on outside.

I was in a bedroom wing with southern exposure, the likely location of the old *señora*'s boudoir. I decided that the old lady would have chosen a large corner room, the one at the end of the wing.

I moved quickly on the strength of the hunch, tried a door, found it unlocked. I left the door open to admit light from outside and let my eyes get used to the gloom.

A wheel chair of lightweight aluminum tubing was standing near the tall windows. I decided this was the place. The bed was vast, sheltered by a canopy on its four posters. The other furniture was as solid as carved stone.

Searching rapidly, I covered the bedroom, the adjoining dressing room and bath, and the little sun-sitting room adjacent on the other side of the huge master room.

Except for the wheel chair, there was no evidence of the old woman's ever having lived here. Not even a loose hairpin in a drawer. The room was a tomb, musty from being closed, without its corpse.

I stood in the middle of the room for a few seconds, thinking about it. They'd certainly wiped out the memory of her, leaving not even a portrait on the walls. And yet . . . neither Keith Sigmon nor Elena had moved into the room. It was almost as if they were afraid of the old woman; or maybe Keith Sigmon was determined to convince himself she had never existed.

I re-entered the hallway and figured how an old lady would have wanted her household arranged. Her secretary-companion must naturally be placed nearby. So I retraced my way a few yards down the hallway and opened a door on a room that had been converted into a sort of combination study and office. There was a desk, a three-drawer filing cabinet, a typewriter on a small metal typewriter table, a matching couch and chair.

None of the filing cabinet or desk drawers was locked. All were empty. The same meticulous vacuum had erased every trace of a girl named Jean Putnam ever having worked here.

I got the pattern. I went into the next room, which I guessed had been Jean Putnam's bedroom, out of force of habit from years of being in my profession.

The pattern wasn't broken. The bedroom had the same lack of sign of human habitation. Nothing in this entire portion of the house remained of the days, weeks, and months when an old woman had hired a very nice young woman to do personal chores.

The honking of a car horn and a burst of laughter drifted to me from outside. I came out of Jean Putnam's bedroom, walked down the hallway to the el, opened a door, and stepped onto the portico.

I was in a shadowed corner, not easily seen. Beyond the courtyard, half a dozen cars were pulling to a stop in the driveway. Laughing, chattering people were spilling out. Several were in costume. The men were pirates or Spanish grandees. The sleek dames were something else again, in *señorita* outfits with cleavage to the belly button, or poured into wispy piratess costumes that looked as if they'd been painted on.

From the way they were already letting down their hair, I guessed the gang was continuing a party that had started with cocktails someplace else. They paused at the bar and began drifting inside, where the musician had got his combo together and given them a downbeat.

I didn't spot Keith and Elena Sigmon right away, and I didn't hang around to do so. I went down the shadowed portico, skirted the courtyard, and headed toward my car.

I was within a few yards of the jalopy when a car stopped near by. Two men and a woman got out. One of the men said, "It's Rivers! . . . Hello, there."

Nervously quick footsteps came toward me. When a man drew closer I saw that it was Van Clavery. Coming forward behind him were his wife and Fred Eppling.

None of the three was in costume. Clavery and the lawyer wore dark business suits. Natalie Clavery had on an expensively simple cocktail dress that gave her a sleek allure not dependent on the exposure of naked flesh.

Clavery looked at me hopefully. "Were you looking for me?"

"Sorry," I said. "I wasn't."

His lean, tense face went swiftly dismal. His sandy brows pulled together. "Seeing you . . . I thought you might have found the old *señora*'s missing brief case."

Natalie Clavery and Fred Eppling reached Clavery's side. We nodded hellos.

"Not yet," I told Clavery. "As a matter of fact, the brief case isn't the only disappearing item."

"What else?"

"A diary," I said. "It belonged to Jean Putnam. It was handed over to Ben McJunkin by Lura Thackery."

Clavery grabbed my arm. "Then you were looking for Lura. Have you talked with her? She might have had a look at whatever Jean had written."

"McJunkin had the same idea," I said. "He reached Lura before I did."

Clavery recoiled, jerking his hand from my arm. Fred Eppling gasped. Natalie Clavery's face turned to carven ivory. In a controlled voice, she said, "Lura is dead?"

"So recently," I said, "it hasn't had time to make the newscasts."

"Is there any doubt that McJunkin did it?"

"I don't think so. He was the tool, the instrument."

"Poor Lura," Natalie said. Her voice had a strange lack of feeling, as if her inner control were taking her beyond human emotion. "She was the 'fraidy-cat, Rivers. She died without ever having really lived."

Very slowly, the cool, sleek woman turned her head to look toward the house. "The brief case, the meaning of all the violence, is still in there."

"You seem very sure," I said.

"Where else?" She faced me directly. "There is a way of making sure."

Her husband was too immersed in his own nerves to notice the hard sheen on her eyes.

Thirteen

Eppling sensed the thing working in her. He glanced at me with concern.

"Have you been in the house?" he said.

I hesitated, then admitted that I had.

"Rivers is a professional," Eppling told Natalie Clavery. "If Van's confession and promissory note were still in there, Rivers would have found them."

She looked at him with a touch of bitterness and contempt. "The Sigmons wouldn't leave such things where even Rivers would find them. But there is a way . . ."

"I'm not Houdini," I conceded. Divorced from my words was a thought: Clavery, take notice and have care with this woman. Clavery, for your sake, your wife has reached the point where she is dangerous.

"Anyway," I added, "I didn't have much time."

"Why not take a little more?" Clavery said, brightening slightly.

"Yes." Eppling nodded. "You might go in as we go."

"Drift into any part of the house you like!" Clavery said.

I looked at the molded perfection of Natalie's profile. "What do you say?"

"I don't think you'll find what you're after."

"It's worth a try," Clavery insisted.

Natalie continued to look at me. "If Keith Sigmon catches you prowling, he'll have you jailed."

"Fred will get a writ," Clavery said. "He'd have you out immediately."

"After facing a man like Ben McJunkin," Eppling said drily, "I don't think jail holds any terrors for Rivers."

I studied Natalie a moment longer; then I turned and headed toward the house.

"Keep it nonchalant," Clavery said nervously. "Nobody's paying any attention to you."

It was true. Most of the guests were drifting inside, toward the savage throbbing of bongos as the drums provided a background for a sensually wailing saxophone. People in the living room were beginning to beat their hands and chant in time to the music.

From the inner part of the courtyard, we were able to see the spectacle inside. Elena Sigmon had claimed the center of the floor and was doing a solo. In a piratess costume covering her like a tight bikini, she was answering the tempo of the insistent drums with writhing twists and turns of her slender, long-legged body.

The beat was gradually and subtly accelerating. Flushed from drink, Elena's small face grew dewy hot with a vicious excitment. She closed her eyes, threw back her head as a frenzied quivering poured through her lithe, firm muscles.

Beyond her, Keith Sigmon killed a drink, tossed the glass to one side. He beat his hands together and yelled encouragement to his daughter. "Do it, baby! Do it!"

Elena responded by pirouetting to tiptoe, arms and body suddenly motionless—except for the unbelievable gyrations of her slender hips.

The guests began to whistle and stamp their feet.

"Now's your chance to slip inside," Clavery said tightly.

I nodded and started toward the shadows of the portico. I was almost out of the lighted area when Elena Sigmon went to the next phase of her routine. Her bare legs flashed as her feet began an intricate pattern of movement.

She spun in a half turn. She suddenly faltered. She jerked to a stop; then whipped back to face again in the direction of the courtyard.

Beside me, a sound of frustration rasped from Clavery. "Don't try it, Rivers," he said, a quick droop in his voice. "Chill it. She's spotted you."

Beyond the tall, open windows, Elena had stood as if recovering from a trance. The lines of her pixie face sharpened, taking the prettiness from the small features. She pushed a couple of people aside as she started from the room, moving toward me. The bongo rhythm hesitated, broke. The high, skirling note of the saxophone dribbled to nothing.

With glances at her and at each other, the guests became uncertain, less at ease. In foggy bewilderment, the first of them followed her into the courtyard. The remainder followed as she planted herself before me.

Under the short, tousled, dark-blond hair, her face was that of a little fox with glittering eyes. "It really is you," she said, getting back her breath after her exertions. "The unforgettable face. When I glimpsed it, I thought for a second I was seeing things."

Her glance passed from me, over Van, Fred, and Natalie. "Did you bring Rivers?" Elena asked coolly.

Equally cool, Natalie said, "We thought the added masculinity would be welcome at your party, my dear."

Elena smiled slyly, dropped a glance at Van, and told

Natalie, "I'm sure masculinity is a quality you'd appreciate."

"The real thing comes in various profiles, sometimes in unsuspected places, my dear."

"Does it really?"

"Oh, yes," Natalie said. "Perhaps one day you'll have the chance to get acquainted with it."

Elena's hand half raised, as if she'd take a dig at Natalie's eyes with her nails. Then she forced her shoulders to relax and gave a soft laugh. "You know how to make with the fancy words, don't you?" The upraised hand reached to pat Natalie's cheek. The suppressed urge to scratch was in the motion. "We're, after all, neighbors and friends and linked by business ties, Mrs. Clavery." Elena spoke with the condescension of the very young for the very old. "We really shouldn't argue, you and I."

Additional guests had arrived, enlarging the group surrounding me in the courtyard. Conversation was buzzing as people wondered what was going on. Even the caterers had drifted toward the promise of excitement.

Keith Sigmon shouldered his way until he was standing before me. He took Elena by the arm, pressuring her aside.

Sigmon's classically chiseled, once-handsome face was pulling its edges tautly together. Some of the whisky fog was clearing from his eyes.

"Rivers, I thought I made it clear——"

"Really, Keith," Natalie Clavery said, "we had no idea his presence would prove such an upsetting——"

"Are you telling me you brought him?"

"Of course."

Sigmon looked at Natalie closely. "I don't believe you,"

he said flatly. "There isn't a reason in the world why you should bring this two-bit private eye to a party."

Van Clavery said with a quietness that got through to me at least, "I'd rather you didn't accuse my wife of being a liar, Keith."

Natalie moved between her husband and Sigmon. As she looked at Sigmon, a brief, secretive expression came to her eyes. "I'm sure Keith didn't mean it that way. Did you?" With a slow curving of her lips and a smoldering upsurge of the thing in her eyes, Natalie gave Sigmon a brief charge of her allure.

Looking at her, he swallowed slowly. "Naturally I meant no offense to you, Van, or Fred."

The buzz of conversation had trickled off. The crowd was restless but quiet, wanting to hear everything that went on. Sigmon was turning toward me. Before he said anything, a voice piped out of the crowd, "That cat came on his own ankles. I'll clue you. He was here before anybody else."

Both Sigmon and I looked toward the speaker. It was the combo leader, simpering under the sudden shift of attention.

"What do you mean?" Sigmon asked in a thick voice.

"Like I have said it, Pops," the musician lighted one of his own breed of cigarettes. "Rivers was making the scene when I got here. We ankled into the house together."

"Are you sure?"

"Pops, like how could I be otherwise? Who could forget that puss?"

Natalie Clavery edged toward Sigmon. "Keith, we saw him and simply didn't want to spoil a party."

He wiped the back of his hand across his high, widow's-peaked forehead. "I understand," he said. "It's okay. But we'll make with a party. A memorable event. A blast to be long remembered."

"Take it easy, Keith," Fred Eppling said.

Sigmon jerked himself away from the lawyer's touch. "Rivers is trespassing. Makes him fair game, doesn't it?"

Sigmon's tone and expression communicated a message to the swarm of guests. Some of them eased fearfully away; other began to crowd in.

"Keith," Eppling tried again, "why don't we talk this over?"

"Nothing more to be said," Sigmon replied. He measured me with his eyes, conscious that every other eye was on him.

Several things didn't have to be spelled out to me. Sigmon was pretty well drunk, dosed with cockiness and false courage, not a good combination for a man whose secret self-doubts must have plagued him for a long time. He was a man who needed to bully others, to break them, to degrade them as in the case of his daughter. A sick man, maybe. But sick like Ben McJunkin.

Unlike McJunkin, Sigmon didn't quite have the guts to create frequent opportunities to strut. The opportunities had to be handed to Sigmon.

He thought he had the opportunity now. He reasoned drunkenly that I was in no position to make an overt move. He was confident that his friends would talk him out of it before it was too late, seize his arms, cajole him.

He put a heavy sneer on his face, which I didn't mind. He took the initial step forward, his hands turning into fists.

I minded. I hit him across the mouth with the back of my right hand. I felt his lips slide across his teeth like banana peels under a heavy rubber heel. A gasp came from the crowd as Sigmon stumbled backward, tripped on his own feet, and fell full length on the flagstones.

He lay there at the feet of all his friends. His face twisted in a grimace of hate. He hated everything and everybody right then, I'm sure. His friends for not having moved on cue. Me for having moved at all.

In the sudden, deep silence, he stared wildly from face to face, shamed and ridiculous, his great moment turned inside out with bitterness and defeat.

I was turning to go. I might have been able to walk away from it. But a man broke the silence with a laugh. A woman giggled. The laughter was contagious.

Then a woman added a new note to the rising laughter. She screamed. This was contagious also. The people began to spill backward, to jostle each other as they attempted to get out of the way.

I spun, saw light glinting on the long blade of the saber that Sigmon had grabbed from one of the Gasparilla pirates. The tip of the blade was reaching to divide my belly button in two parts.

I sucked in breath, twisted to one side, and folded my body out of the way.

The rush from the center of the action became chaotic. I heard a man trip and fall into the courtyard fountain. In the perimeter of my gaze, I saw a woman get stepped on as she fainted dead away.

These were secondary impressions. Anything other than the sight of the long steel blade was secondary.

Sigmon's rush had carried him past me. He was turning, the saber swinging up. It was no toy but the genuine article, probably an antique sword with a real history of pirate blood. A little something extra for the owner to keep shined up for the day each year when the owner put on his pirate's costume.

Sigmon's drunken sense of outrage had passed the point of sanity. He was beyond knowing or caring that I might shoot him. Nothing was real to him right now except the face of a hated man who had humbled him.

I ducked under his two-handed swinging of the saber, heard the swish of it. Before he could get the weapon set for another try at laying the side of my face open, I drove in low and hard.

My shoulder hit him, and I discovered he was as soft in the gut as I'd thought. I felt the air rush out of him and heard the muffled scream it left in his throat.

His body folded across my back. He went backward, and I fell on top of him.

I shook free of him and got to my feet. Clutching his stomach, he rolled back and forth a time or two. Then in the upper stratum of queazy sickness and pain, he saw the hovering outlines of my face.

His face twisted in raw fear, he scrabbled himself around, got his hands and knees under him, and started crawling away.

The target was too exposed, the temptation too great. I drew back my foot, and kicked him squarely in the tail. The force of it knocked him flat again, on his face this time. His fingers clawed at the flagstones as he tried to pull himself beyond my reach.

He needn't have worried. He wasn't worth further bother. I bent, touched the saber where it had clattered to rest. I picked the weapon up, studied it a moment while the hushed faces scattered around the courtyard watched.

Gripping the saber by the tip and haft, I raised my

knee and brought the sword down across it. The way it rang when it snapped attested the quality of the steel.

I pitched the pieces of broken saber. They struck flagstones near Keith Sigmon with a clatter.

I turned and walked away. As I passed from the lighted area of the courtyard, I heard the timorous return of life back there. Rustling movement. The sound of voices.

Sigmon was being helped to his feet. Elena was suggesting drinks all around.

Fingers began falling on a bongo like warm, fat, tropical raindrops.

Fourteen

When I got back to my car I saw the shadowy outlines of a person in the front seat. The dome light turned on as I opened the door on the driver's side.

Myrtle Higgins leaned across the seat, looking up at me. A smile curved her full, red lips. "Hi," she said casually.

With her firm-cheeked face and full-breasted, amazonian body, she was a pervasive presence that took some of the tension out of my shoulders. I slipped under the wheel beside her. Half-turned, she rested with her elbow on the back of the seat. "You know something," she said, her voice suddenly serious, touched with a feeling akin to fright, "old José Gaspar would never have taken you in his crew."

"No?"

"It would have cost him sleep, worrying about you breaking him in two and taking command."

I looked at the lusty, surface perfection of her physical shell. "I wish I knew you better."

"Remember the other night," she said softly. "How much better can a man know a woman?"

"You know what I'm talking about. I don't know you at all. Not the Myrtle Higgins who waits and hides behind the eyes."

"Don't talk like that," she said, straightening in the seat.

"Okay," I said. I gave her a glance. "Going to the party?"

"Maybe. Or maybe I've been rambling around, looking for you."

"So now you've found me."

"Sure—and who wants to go to Elena Sigmon's silly party?" Her smile was back. She was trying for a mood of casual ease, lightness. "I got here in time to see the finish of the fight after I'd spotted your car. Don't you think we'd better get away from here?"

"Why?"

"Sigmon has grounds to swear out a warrant for you."

"I don't think Sigmon wants any cops around," I said.

"Let's get moving anyway." She stirred restlessly. "I need to move, to talk, Ed."

I started the car, turned it around, and followed the headlights through the warmly dark jungle landscaping.

"Ed . . . I heard about Lura Thackery on a newscast."

"I'll feel bad about that one a long time," I said.

She looked at me quickly. "You shouldn't. The girl was a fool. She brought it on herself."

"Did you know her well, Myrtle?"

"Not very. Just as a friend of Jean Putnam's who came to the hacienda occasionally to see Jean. Old Señora Isabella didn't much like to have Lura around."

"Why not?"

"Oh, I don't know," Myrtle said. "I think Lura reminded the old lady of her own daughter."

"In what way?"

"They were both weak," Myrtle said. "The old woman regarded her daughter's marriage and subjection to Keith Sigmon as the height of human weakness and folly."

I reached the boulevard and waited for a break in traffic.

"Anything personal between the old woman and Lura Thackery?" I asked.

"Not that I know of. The *señora* was courteous to Lura. She was too well versed in the social graces not to be. But she was always distant with the girl, as if her wise old instincts were solidly set against Lura."

I gunned the car and shot onto the boulevard.

"Got a cigarette?" Myrtle said.

I handed her a package, pressed the car lighter.

"As the old woman's nurse," I said, "you were probably closer to her than anyone in Tampa."

"I wouldn't be sure. There was her doctor—and Jean Putnam. I think Jean was the closest of all. Jean seemed to fill a little of the inner void the old woman had brought with her from Venezuela."

"But even Jean didn't see and talk with the *señora* in moments of pain, in the small hours when she was suffering."

Myrtle watched the sweep of lights and darkness. "Part of a nurse's job, Ed," she said quietly.

"So you heard words from her that not even Jean Putnam ever heard."

She stirred, turning partially toward me. "What do you want of me, Ed?"

"I'm not sure. A word, maybe, that the old woman spoke when the night was deep and the pain was heavy."

"I wish I had a word, Ed."

"Or a fact. A detail that hasn't come to light yet."

The lustrous dark-blond hair swished about the fine wide shoulders. "I can give you much, Ed. You've only to name it. But I'm not able to give you anything in the realm of your work."

"You knew them," I said, "all the people around the old lady. One of them, back there at the party tonight, is a murderer."

"Ben McJunkin . . ."

"The tool," I said. "Nothing less, nothing more."

I pressed the brake pedal and we became one of the cars massing at a row of traffic signals. "You see how it is," I said. "Ben McJunkin is operating on his own terms. If he comes to me again, I may not live to get to the person behind him. If I reach the person behind McJunkin first, then I can go to McJunkin. The odds would be a little better that way."

"My God, Ed! Do you have to keep talking about it?"

"Want to go back to the party?"

"Oh, you . . ." She seethed. She jerked herself to the far side of the seat. Her huff didn't last long. She sighed almost wearily. "I'm no detective, Ed. I don't know how to play detective."

"You knew the people. You're no fool. You've dealt with people a long time in extreme circumstances. You know what to look for."

"In a murderer?" she demanded. "How was I to suspect that one of them was planning to silence Jean Putnam and Lura Thackery?"

"Okay," I said. "I guess I was just trying to strike my last match in a high wind."

"What am I supposed to say?" she cried. "Keith and Elena Sigmon? I hardly know them. Van Clavery? A nervous wreck on two legs who probably wakes up with ants in his pants and goes to bed seething from all the real and fancied mistakes of the day. He burned with envy for the old *señora*'s wealth and position. But he liked Jean Putnam.

"Ditto for Fred Eppling. Cold fish of a lawyer. Got a high yearly retainer from the old lady, although his tasks were mostly routine. Untangled one minor legal snarl for her in Caracas, but mostly never had to leave his office except to come to her home. He got Jean Putnam her job with Señora Isabella, remember—but if he had any wish to see Jean dead, it's beyond my imagination.

"Natalie Clavery? A glistening object of art made out of alabaster. But plenty of hot blood under the cool surface. Deep down, she's a tigress, the kind that takes a mate without reservation—and who knows what sort of specimen the chemistry of a woman will react to?"

"Part of the wondrous mystery of women," I said.

"Sure." She looked at me obliquely. "Take my own case. Here I am—with a big, sweaty hulk who borrowed the shoulders from a gorilla, got his daintiness from a bull, and dredged up the face from the left-overs when

Mother Nature put a wrestler together. Here I am—of my own free will. Maybe I really should have my head examined!"

"Don't start thinking objectively about me," I said, "just about those other people."

"I've given you everything I can, Ed, and I'm sure it's nothing you didn't already know. So why not forget it for a little while? Give yourself a chance to simmer down, relax. Buy me a drink."

"The bars are awfully crowded."

"Who said anything about a bar?" she asked.

While we were going up the stairs to my apartment, I heard the phone ringing. I murmured "Pardon" to Myrtle, hurried up the remainder of the stairway, and keyed the door open. Even if the phone was demanding attention, I reached around the door frame and clicked on a light before I took the final steps into the bed-sitting room.

The phone lapsed to silence as I reached it. I said, "Hello?" to a humming dial tone.

I dropped the phone slowly back in its hooks. When I turned, Myrtle was standing in the doorway.

"The caller get tired and hang up, Ed?"

I nodded. "If it's important, maybe they'll call back."

She crossed the room, touched my arm with her hand, urged me to one side as I started into the kitchenette.

"I know where the makings are," she said. "Unbutton your collar and sit down. Beer chaser?"

"Just beer," I said.

She raised her brows slightly and went on into the kitchenette.

I wandered back to the phone, picked it up, and tried

the answering service. There had been no calls downtown. Just here, on the line into my domestic domain.

I was standing there frowning at the phone when Myrtle crossed the room, set beer and whisky on the table, and slipped her arms loosely about my neck.

"You're still not with me, Ed. Forget the call. Probably some anemic chick who'd stack up against me like a sack of sticks."

I pulled her closer to me. The warm pressure of her breasts and thighs against me was firm, but imbued with a heady female plasticity.

"You know," I said, "that if you'd ever entered a Miss Universe contest the nursing profession would have lost a member."

"Your beer's getting warm."

"Not only the beer."

She laughed, cupped my face in her hands, tilted her head, and gave me a warmly moist kiss.

I slid my fingers up through the silken wealth of dark-tan hair, and returned the gesture.

We stood there with our lips and bodies welding together and soft little sounds forming in her throat. Anything beyond this building, this room, this one spot began not to matter.

The phone rang.

We drew apart slowly. The phone started its second shrill peal for attention.

"Don't answer it, Ed."

"You know I have to. Anyway, it's barely past dinnertime. The evening's young."

In irritation, she jerked away and walked halfway across the room.

I picked up the phone. "Hello?" I said.

"Ed Rivers?" The accent was Spanish.

"Yes."

"Where do you keep yourself? I have been calling again and again."

"Who is this?"

"Pepe Tortugas, who runs the bar."

"Long time no see."

"*Sí*, Señor Ed, not since you cleared my brother of the armed-robbery charge more than a year ago."

"You paid me for the chore, Pepe."

"But I have long felt that money was very cold payment, *señor*. My brother . . . he works now every day. The prospect of prison worked a change in him. Now I have the chance to do something for you." He paused, took a breath, called on his courage. "I understand you have been seeking an individual."

"Yes," I said, a tightness crawling into my throat. "Yes, I have."

"You try the San Salvador Hotel, room four-oh-four."

"I will."

"You must not ask me how I know this, Señor Ed. I would have to lie to you. I have no wish to do that."

"No questions, Pepe."

"We in bars overhear many things. We are told things by lips loose from alcohol."

"I understand, Pepe. You have no need to worry. No one will ever know where my information came from."

"*Gracias, señor*. One more thing, he has watchful friends who will warn him of activity, of the police. He will not return to the room, if warned. You will fail—and perhaps not again have the chance to locate him."

"I see," I said, a brief pulse moving through my gut.

"I wish it could be different for you, Señor Ed. But tasks do not always arrange themselves most conveniently. When it is all over, stop by my bar. A drink on the house will be waiting."

Fifteen

When I turned from the phone, Myrtle was studying me carefully. Her eyes went a shade darker. Her lips became redder and heavier as the background skin turned whiter. She shook her head from side to side, the dark-blond hair splashing across her cheeks. "No," she said softly. "No, no, no!"

I slid the .38 from under the waistband of my pants and started checking it. I had a replacement blade for the one McJunkin had carried out of here the other night in his tissues, but I wasn't counting on the knife at all now. McJunkin had already had experience with it.

Myrtle took a slow step toward me, unable to tear her gaze from my face. "I won't let you go, Ed!"

"I have to go."

"With the police?"

"It won't work that way," I said. "I need—and want—to do this one alone."

"Where is McJunkin, Ed?"

"On the moon."

"I'm no dainty-fingered hothouse plant! Don't treat me like one!"

"Just wait here," I said. "You can drink your drink."

"I don't want a drink. Not now. I'm going with you."

"You're nuts, Myrtle."

"I won't sit and wait. So help me, Ed, I won't just sit."

"Then try the TV. They're broadcasting a Gasparilla beauty pageant on a local station tonight."

As I moved, she reversed directions, going backward, keeping herself between me and the door.

"Who called you, Ed?"

"A man named Pepe."

"There are a million Pepes!"

"Just a few thousand in Ybor City. Anyway, it wouldn't do you any good if you knew which Pepe. You couldn't trace me that way. He'd tell you nothing."

The door pressed against her back. Tears came to her eyes. "You want me to beg, Ed?"

"You know I don't."

Her moist gaze worked into every detail of my face. A faint change came to her, a hint of the depths beyond the molded surface perfection. For a second the physical shell was almost lifted to the plane of rare beauty.

"Cut it out," I said. "You're not looking at me for the last time."

"You're a fool, Ed."

I touched her shoulder. "Don't make me push you to one side."

"You'll have to if you go. Why do you have to be such a fool!"

"Give me an alternative," I said. "I want an alternative. I'm a scared fool looking for an alternative."

The force of my hand increased, sliding her across the face of the door. There was resistance in her; then it melted out of her.

As I opened the door, she said bitterly, "Your mother should have had an abortion!" She wheeled away, crossed the room, and picked up her drink. She was working on it seriously when I closed the door behind me.

The crowded streets, the lights, the sounds of a city at play slid by the car as the minutes passed. Then ahead was an old neon with some of the letters dead and others quivering. The glass tubing spelled out "San Salvador Hotel."

I parked a block away, around the next corner. I sat there for a minute or two with thoughts running through my head, the weight of the .38 against my belly, and the desire not to get out of the car strong inside me.

I got out, felt the pavement beneath my feet, and watched the car door swing closed.

I walked slowly but without hesitation to the corner. Traffic swished endlessly. A group of laughing young people came out of a club, flowed around me, and chattered in Spanish while they waited for the light to change.

It's fifty-fifty, I thought. McJunkin is either in his room right now, or he isn't. I don't want him to be. I want him to be out munching beans and peppers or working on a steak. I want him to walk into the room and find me there. And this is the best time of day to take the chance. No calling the hotel or asking any questions that will be brought to his attention and give him warning. Straight to his room. Play the odds. Pretty favorable odds, at that. If he's there, he won't know anyone is coming.

If it isn't a trap . . . If he didn't get to Pepe Tortugas and force Pepe to make the call . . . No . . . Pepe *sounded* right. There is a sound a man makes when a gun is at his head.

While my brain kicked thoughts around like french fries in a deep frier of boiling grease, my feet took me casually toward the San Salvador. As I went past, I studied the lobby without turning my head. It was the rundown showplace of a once-fine hotel. The chandelier was grimy and partly lighted. The potted palms were dusty, with missing fronds. The ancient leather couches and chairs showed lumps and low places. The gloomy and bedraggled room was empty except for an old man working behind the desk.

A few yards beyond the hotel a dark alley formed a break between the buildings. I walked quietly into the alley, went twenty yards, and stood with my back against the rough brick side of the hotel where the shadows combined to form a pool of absolute blackness.

I made the best possible use of the next ten minutes by staying perfectly still and watching the mouth of the alley.

Satisfied that no one had noticed me enter, I moved deeper into the alley. A very few of the rooms overhead were lighted. From one came the sound of two old geezers in sudden argument. I translated enough of their Spanish to gather that they were about to come to blows over a game of dominoes.

They kept at it, getting a little louder. It began to bug me. Shut up, I thought; it isn't that important . . . Go back to your game . . . Two old men come to blows and the cops come . . . Cops come and Ben McJunkin doesn't come home tonight . . .

You see how it was, how it goes. You move into the warped world of the Ben McJunkins and nothing remains quite normal. The argument of two old men you've never seen can postpone a meeting tonight, and tomorrow may be too late. Tomorrow McJunkin might have figured a way to get to you.

I looked up at the lighted window, lips thinned and flat against my teeth. In the manner of Spaniards, the two old men stopped it as suddenly as they had begun it. Quietness returned to the alley.

"Thanks," I muttered in the direction of the window two stories overhead.

I started moving again, locating the service door a few yards farther on. Without striking a light I explored the lock with my fingertips. It was old, as old as the building. Opening the lock would have been duck soup—but there were heavy studs near it, indicating a chain or heavy bolt inside.

With the back door ruled out, I reversed my field a few steps and paused at the fire escape. The prospect of using it didn't make me happy. I had to go four stories up. During that time, I'd be limned against the night sky. The odds were very long against it, but no guarantee that someone passing on the street wouldn't glance down the alley and see the shadow of a prowling man on the escape.

I flexed my knees and leaped upward with hands raised high. My fingers were short of their goal by inches. I landed with a soft thud. I took a moment to relax my arm and leg muscles. I put a real punch behind the next jump.

Rough metal touched my fingers. My body was swinging clear of the ground. The hinged counterbalanced section of the escape began to lower under my weight.

The end of the section thudded to rest on the alley. I stood on the steel slats of the bottom step to keep the counter weight from raising the section. I didn't move right away, listening to make sure the soft but unusual sounds had attracted no attention.

I moved up to the first landing, taking my handkerchief in my hand. I used the handkerchief for a pad as I grasped the weathered braided metal cable that ran through a pulley to connect the counter weight to the free-swinging end of the escape.

Braking the pull of the weight, I let the swinging bottom section rise silently to a horizontal position. Again I waited, my back pressed against the building there at first-floor level.

With the alley continuing quiet and peaceful, I started up. I stayed close to the building where I was less likely to be seen and where the old metal of the escape protested least under my weight. As I climbed, flakes of rust shivered loose from the thin steel webbing and trickled in little showers to the alley below. The rust motes struck with the grainy sound of sifting sand, but to my heightened senses, it sounded like bricks were falling.

When I reached the fourth-floor level I experienced the luxury of a long, deep breath. A feeble corridor light glowed beyond the window, which was open against the warmth. A sluggish breeze stirred, billowing the edges of grayish curtains through the window.

I let the curtain edge catch on my finger and took a look inside. The corridor was short, an emergency exit connecting to the main hallway.

I put my rump on the window sill, swung my legs across, and ducked in. When the hotel had basked proudly in its shine of newness, the carpeting had been superb, wall to wall, padded thickly. Now it was threadbare, composed in part of dust that had accumulated over the years. It still deadened the sound of footfalls.

I endured a tight moment as I stepped into the main hallway, which was at right angles to the service hall. Overhead a small red light marked the emergency exit.

I turned to the left, making a random choice. Glancing at the numbers on the first two doors I passed, I saw that they got higher.

I turned and started in the other direction, toward 404. A door opened just in front of me. A woman came out of her room, gave me hardly a glance, went to the elevator, and punched a button. I heard the faint reverberations as the ancient self-service elevator rattled upward.

I reached 404 but didn't stop. I walked to the far end of the corridor, came to a halt, and went through the motions of a man searching for keys.

The stinking elevator was bumbling toward its destination by inches. The woman was beginning to be aware of me, looking away quickly when I glanced at her.

I made as if I was fitting a key in the door and the elevator finally reached the end of its journey. Hesitant creaks marked the opening of the elevator door. The woman got aboard, and the cage started down.

Alone in the corridor, I spun and moved to McJunkin's room. A thin sweat spread a cold touch across my forehead. I slid my hand to the waistband of my pants and curled my fingers around the butt of the .38.

Sixteen

I knocked on the door matter-of-factly.

I listened for the rustle of a bed spring, the pad of a foot. I waited for him to say, "Who's there?"

If he was in the room, I was set to snap the lock and kick the door open, using my heel as a pile driver. I was ready to show him the business end of the .38 before he had a chance to do a thing about it.

Nothing happened. I tried again, laying my knuckles a little harder against the door, just in case he was in the john and hadn't heard the first knock.

The room and hallway remained silent. The sweat on my face felt as if a brief ray of sunlight had touched it. He'd had everything his own way so far, been able to call the shots. I was past due for a break.

While I still enjoyed solitude in the hallway, I slipped the key ring from my pocket and separated the thin steel from the keys. I worked the steel carefully into a hairline crack where the door molding was attached. I watched the steel disappear, felt it make contact with the beveled metal latch of the spring lock.

Applying pressure, I sensed the spring beginning to yield. The steel was sliding across the sloping end of the latch, forcing it back. It clicked softly.

Leaving the steel where it was to keep the latch from jumping back into its hasp, I turned the doorknob. The door opened quietly. I removed the steel and returned it to my pocket.

I slid inside the room, closed the door, letting the lock function.

I stood a moment while my eyes got used to the dim illumination that came from outside neon and streetlight glow.

Probing with a miniature pocket flashlight, I started a circuit of the layout. Physically, the surroundings were what I'd expected, typical drab room in a drab hotel. The furnishings were heavy, solid, but old and scarred and scorched in spots from careless cigarettes. The counterpane and curtains were limp and dingy. Water gathered lazily and dripped from worn faucets in the bathroom.

I let the thin finger of light linger in the bathroom washbasin. There were stains in the bottom of the pitted porcelain bowl. Not rust stains. Someone had built a small fire in the basin and later washed away whatever had been burned. I wondered if it had been Jean Putnam's diary.

Coming from the bath, I crossed the bedroom to the closet and swung the door open. Like the rest of the abode, the closet reflected the habits of a man reasonably neat and orderly in his personal habits. Suits and slacks were carefully hung. On the floor were two pairs of shoes, clean and modestly shined.

As I swung the suits aside, the light beam jerked up short. In the back of the closet was a woman's silk print dress. Next to it was a very sheer black negligee with filmy lace across the bosom, a garment designed to enhance erotic play.

I found the remainder of her things at the chest of drawers, a few of her cosmetics tidily arranged on top, changes of panties, bras, hose, and shoes in the uppermost drawer. The remainder of the chest was given over to McJunkin's apparel—shirts, underwear, socks. The two bottom drawers were empty.

Whoever she was, I decided, she didn't live here full time, not unless she had a very skimpy wardrobe. I pegged her as a regular visitor who'd left here the bare necessities to freshen up.

From the chest, the flashlight ray swung to the bedside table. Next to the lamp was a stack of folded newspapers, the accumulation of several days. The top one was creased to expose an account of Jean Putnam's murder. I lifted the first paper. The one beneath told the tale of the death by violence of Lura Thackery. McJunkin's bedtime reading when he didn't have a visitor to entertain him . . .

A shrill bell chattered suddenly in the silence. As I turned, the flash beam pinwheeled to come to rest on the bureau where the phone reposed. The old man on the switchboard at the desk downstairs gave it a long try, paused, and let the phone blast a second time.

Then he must have told the caller that McJunkin wasn't in his room. The phone didn't ring again.

I resumed movement, flicking the light into the wastebasket, which was snugged against the wall beside the bureau.

With the barrel of the .38, I pushed aside laundry shirt wrappers, discarded magazines. Near the bottom of the container I saw red leatherette.

Bending a little lower, I dipped my hand all the way and pulled out the covers of a small book. I slapped the dust of old cigarette ashes from it, laid it face down on the bureau, and played the light over it. The entire contents had been ripped out. On the broken and bent leatherette cover were two initials in gold: J. P.

While I was standing there looking at the remains of Jean Putnam's diary, I heard a key rattle in the lock. I peeled around from the bureau and put the dingy wallpaper against my back. I turned off the miniature flash and dropped it in my pocket as he twisted his key in the lock.

The door swung open, covering me. He entered the room with heavy, solid footsteps.

The muscles across my belly pulled flat and hard. A faint singing sensation flowed along my nerves as Mc-Junkin's bulk came into view.

He'd heeled the door closed, reached for the light switch, the movement turning him squarely away from me. The door latch and light switch clicked simultaneously.

While his hand was still on the switch, I put the barrel of the .38 against the nape of his neck.

"Friend," I said, "if the wheel keeps turning, a new number is bound to come up."

He held it right there, his half-twisted, arm-extended position having some of the aspects of a Rodin statue.

"Rivers," he said.

"Check."

I patted his armpits and kidneys. He wore a revolver in a shoulder holster on his left side. I reached around him, lifted the gun, and jammed it in my hip pocket.

Energy and sensation began returning to his muscles. He turned slowly and carefully. For the first time we were face to face. His mug shots had been accurate. He was big, rangy, flat-bellied. With a strong-boned, good-looking face marred only by the thin white scar along his jawbone, he looked like a one-time college football player—which he was—who'd gone on to reach middle age in a rugged, outdoors field of endeavor—which he hadn't.

The thinning brown hair over the broad forehead caught the light dully. The hazel eyes reflected it like hard, polished chips of resin.

"You'd better make the most of this," he said quietly. "You won't be telling any grandchildren about it."

"We'll see."

"I'm not alone, you know."

"My primary interest," I said. "We'll talk about this person who made the contract with you."

"What contract?" He turned toward the bureau and reached for a cigarette package. I hit him across the knuckles with the gun barrel. He jerked his hand back. An expression of pain flicked across his face. Then he laughed thinly, lifted his knuckles to his mouth, and sucked off the flecks of blood.

"You can do this any way you like, McJunkin. The hard way. The reasonable way."

He gave me a hooded glance, walked to the bed, and sat on the edge of it. With the long years of experience behind him, he was cool and collected. He'd been in and out of too many tight spots to believe in the finality of defeat.

"You're not talking to a punk kid, Rivers."

"You convinced me of that at the very start," I said.

"I got rights."

"Have you? I remember seeing your rights carted off in the meat wagon, McJunkin."

He sat brooding. "I ought to castrate the sonofabitch who gave you this room number."

I put the gun barrel under his chin and tipped his head up.

"Glom the truth, McJunkin. You've dealt with lenient or corrupt judges, charitable juries, do-gooders on parole boards for so long you feel the ultimate disaster can't really happen to you. It can. It has."

"What will it get you? It won't bring the dead chicks back."

"Then they'll have company, McJunkin."

"And where will you be?"

"Around," I said.

"Not for long. There are others like me, and plenty of money to hire them. You got icky ideas, Rivers, a cluckhead way of looking at things."

"Coming from you, thanks for the compliment."

"I'm thinking of the best thing for everybody." He swallowed against the pressure of the gun barrel. "It's not too late. You want your tail in a coffin or sitting on velvet? I can talk to my principal. I think I can swing it. Nobody wants to keep this thing stirred up. The quicker we close the book on it, the better."

"I'm hard of hearing, McJunkin."

"The ailment can be fixed."

"Are you the doctor?"

"Why not?" he said. "Just repeat what Jean Putnam and Lura Thackery said to you. Mention how long Jean was able to talk before she died."

"How much do you think she talked?"

"Not much," he said. "She didn't spell it out, or you'd have broken it by now. But the catch is, she reached you. She started you on the Claverys and the Sigmons. She got you into it, and as long as you're in it, you're dangerous. It's a chance we can't take."

"You've no choice left about taking chances, McJunkin."

"I think you got it twisted, friend. I'm offering you a brand-new, and very final chance. To step aside. To do nothing. How many people can set a price on doing nothing?"

"I like to stay busy," I said.

"Be busy in style. Write your own ticket. Buy yourself a dozen chicks. Take a trip around the world."

Very gently, he lifted his hand, touched my wrist, eased the force of the gun barrel from his chin.

"Think about it for a minute," he said. "We're professionals, you and me. We sell the same products, nerve and muscle and service."

"To a different clientele, McJunkin. For different reasons."

"Okay. I won't argue the point. You work one side of the street; I work the other. We lock horns: it's in the line of business. Nothing personal. You shoot at a guy one day; maybe you want to protect him the next. Depends on the setup. All a matter of business."

"Think I need your protection, McJunkin?"

"Maybe we got a mutual need, mutual interests. There's more money involved than you could count in half a dozen lifetimes, Rivers. A little of the small change will set you up for a long time to come."

"For doing nothing," I said.

"Just change teams, Rivers."

"You got worms in the wrinkles of your brain, McJunkin."

"Then I got the most plentiful parasites in the world. Only difference is, I don't hide mine behind fancy words and a hypocritical front. I'm what I am, Rivers, and I never go back on a deal. You can trust me when it comes to business. Once you're in, we'll have to trust each other."

"No sale, McJunkin."

The hazel eyes clouded with confusion, the inability to comprehend that it all wasn't as clear and reasonable to me as it was to him.

"Maybe I didn't make this clear," he said.

"Very."

"Then I don't dig," he said. "Right now, whatever you do to me, you got a one-way ticket to nowhere. You can trade it for plush. What's holding you back?"

"If you were capable of understanding, McJunkin, you wouldn't need an explanation."

"Man, what else can I say?"

"One word," I said.

He shook his head. A quiet sadness came to his husky face. "You know I can't."

"His name, McJunkin. Or hers."

"I made a deal, Rivers."

"I'm unmaking it," I said. "My only out is to reach your principal before a parade of McJunkins stops me from being a danger."

"I offered you the smart way out. You're too dumb to like money."

"I like it very much," I said, "but not as much as my own life. You offered me a sure way to set myself up. The choice isn't mine—but yours. Which will it be? Me? Or your principal?"

He seemed to pull down inside of himself, becoming a dumb animal prepared to endure suffering. His answer was in his silence.

Seventeen

I reached toward him to grab his collar. In reaching, I leaned forward. In leaning, I saved my life.

The gun winked on the roof of the building across the alley. Shards of glass from the window of McJunkin's room spilled to the floor like dimes from an up-ended pocket. The sound was immediately followed by the spilling of glass from the bureau mirror as the slug crossed the spot where I had been standing.

I dropped, hit the floor, and rolled away. McJunkin crossed the room and struck the light switch. The return of intense gloom blinded me for a moment.

I fired the .38, realizing almost instantly that the shot was high. His body was a shadow that had dropped into a crouch in anticipation of the shot.

He'd grabbed the end of the dresser. Shoving with all his power, he fired it straight at me, its small metal casters rolling with a quick, angry, hollow sound.

I threw up my arm to keep the end of the rushing bureau from knocking my brains out. Twisting, I took most of the force against my shoulder. Off balance, I was slammed against the wall by the impact.

I kicked the piece of furniture aside as McJunkin threw the latch and eeled through the door. The hallway light caught him. I had time to fire once as he was slamming the door behind him.

I knew I had hit him. The slug knocked him halfway around. Then the door had boomed closed between us.

I started to rise, ducked again as the gun across the alley fired three times, the bullets searching the room at random. The nature of the volley indicated to me that it would be the last. Whoever was over there would get off the roof quickly and out of an unhealthy neighborhood.

I scrambled to my feet, lunged across the room, and yanked McJunkin's door open. I glanced toward the elevator, saw the stairwell beside it.

As I headed for the stairs, I glanced up to check the elevator pointer. It told me the cage was at ground level. McJunkin hadn't been able to use it.

I plunged into the stairwell and started down. I was carrying the .38 openly. Marked by knife and gun, McJunkin was proving that he had the durability of a razorback tusker. I didn't want to kill him. I wanted him to talk. If I had to maim him seriously to keep him in speaking distance, I was prepared to do so.

I passed the third-floor landing without seeing any sign of him. I continued down with my feet knocking puffs of dust from the ancient stair runner.

Second-floor level. The stairs remained empty before me.

First floor.

It was impossible. He could not have come down any faster than I had.

The old deskman was stricken to a state of semi-paralysis as he watched my rush across the lobby.

His eyes were hard on the gun when I stopped at the desk.

"I . . . I . . . I . . ." he said.

"Take it easy, Pop. I'm not going to hurt you."

He clutched the edge of the desk. Under wispy white

brows his eyes rolled upward until the irises were half hidden.

I reached across the desk, gripped his arm gently to support him. "Don't faint on me, Pop. Nothing's going to happen to you. Which way did McJunkin go?"

"Muh . . . muh . . . muh . . . Muhjunkin?"

"You must have noticed him hightailing it across the lobby," I said. "When he hit the street, which way did he turn?"

The old man's senses had pulled back from the brink. The reaction of it brought high color to his white, sunken cheeks and broke sweat across his lined forehead.

I gave his arm a little shake. "Come on, Pop. I need every second. The man's a murderer."

"Murderer?"

"McJunkin, damn it!"

"McJunkin?"

"The big man from four-o-four," I said.

"That's Rogers."

"I don't care what name he registered under. Which direction did he pick?"

"I didn't see him."

"You couldn't have missed him, Pop."

"I saw him come in—but not out. Rogers . . . McJunkin, you say? He came in and gave me that very nice smile of his, like always. Not many do, you know. It's like I'm a piece of furniture, but he always spoke and asked me how I was feeling. He rode the elevator up, several minutes ago, and I haven't seen him since." The old man raised a finger and thoughtfully picked his nose. "If you're a cop, better show me some credentials and start explaining. Rogers don't seem to be like no killer. He's a cut above what we usually . . ."

I let the old man deliver the remainder of the character reference to my backside as I hurried out of the lobby. On the street, Gasparilla merriment was being expressed in a torchlight parade complete with hobgoblins, skeletons, mobs of pirates. Squawkers and noisemakers created a chaotic tide of sound. Against the riotous din, the popping of a pistol four stories away would have been as noticeable as the crunch of a peanut shell.

With the .38 out of sight under my shirt, I used my hands and elbows to push my way through the swarms of people. Reaching the alley, I was free of the entangling mass.

I slid my hand under my shirt to touch the gun and ran toward the hotel fire escape.

I paused close to the building, saw no movement in the alley.

Sliding the miniature flashlight from my pocket, I pointed the beam upward. Close to the side of the building, the counterweight was still swaying on its rusty cable below the pulley. McJunkin, I knew, had reached the bottom of the fire escape mere minutes ago, imparting force to the counterweight when he'd stepped to the ground, the departure of his weight permitting the bottom section of the escape to swing back up to its usual position when not in use.

A feeling of wild rage came over me. I looked toward the mouth of the alley, at the carefree swirl of humanity in which McJunkin had lost himself. I had the reasonless urge to smash something.

Then I dragged in a deep, deliberate breath and scanned the area around my feet with the flashlight beam. I found the first glistening red glob of blood near the base of the fire escape. A trail of crimson droplets, spaced a few yards apart, pointed toward the street.

I jostled my way through the sidewalk throngs, returning to the lobby of the hotel. The old man was standing in the doorway. He looked at me uncertainly. I brushed past him, crossed to the phone booth, and shut myself in.

With the phone in my hand, I hesitated. Then I shrugged and dropped a coin in the slot. I dialed Lieutenant Steve Ivey's home number. He answered on the third ring.

I cleared my throat. "Ed Rivers, Steve."

"What's up?"

"Plenty. I had a face-to-face chat with Ben McJunkin at the San Salvador Hotel."

"Have you got him? What does he say?"

"I had him," I said, "but a friend of his fire-escaped to the top of the neighboring building and started taking pot shots. I didn't have a chance to finish talking with McJunkin."

I sensed the build-up of an explosion as Ivey hunted words.

"Don't light into me, Steve," I cautioned. "My own fuse has burned damn short. I suggest you blanket this area and alert all local doctors. McJunkin will have to have medical attention. He's hurt badly this time. Not a flesh wound from a knife, either. He's carrying a bullet."

I hung up before Ivey started tongue-lashing me for being a bad boy. I saw no sense in the waste of time.

Myrtle Higgins had waited with my apartment door open. When she heard my footsteps coming up, she rushed to the top of the stairs. She stood looking down at me, a lush Valkyrie swaying slightly and reaching for the newel post to steady herself.

I hurried up the remaining steps and caught her around the waist. She leaned against me, resting her face on my shoulder. I felt the beating of her heart.

"You . . . you made it," she said.

"Did you expect me not to?"

"I didn't know," she said. "This waiting has been hell, Ed."

"You need a drink."

"No, not now." She eased away from me, brushed the tangle of heavy, dark-blond hair from the side of her face. "I can manage under my own steam."

She moved into the apartment ahead of me. "Did you find Ben McJunkin?"

"Yes."

"What happened?"

"I shot him."

She gasped, looked at me, shivered slightly. "Did you kill him?"

"No."

"Then . . . it isn't over?"

"Not quite," I said. "He got away. But we'll get him this time. From signs I saw in the alley where he escaped, McJunkin will either have to reach a doctor or bleed to death."

She touched my cheek, let her hand fall. "I think I will go home, Ed. I feel . . . limp."

"I'm a little dishraggish myself," I admitted, "but a beer should be of some very slight help. Sure you won't join me?"

She shook her head. "The pirates can have the city tonight. For me, a long, hot bath, a good book. When the book gets tiresome I'll have a sleeping pill. I hope I don't have bad dreams. You've put me through a lot this evening."

"Sorry."

"Don't be, Ed. Ben McJunkin was to blame." She picked up her small handbag and crossed the room to the wall mirror. I watched her run a comb through her hair and touch a lipstick to her mouth.

"I intend to crash a party," I said. "It may be interesting. Sure you won't reconsider and join me?"

"Nope. The party mood has been wrung out of me. Cold water seems to have been dashed over the lovely fire."

"Too bad."

Our gazes met in the mirror. "There's always the prospect of another evening, Ed. The future holds a lot of nights."

"I suppose so," I said. "Well, if this is the way it's got to be, I'll take you home."

"Go ahead and crash your party. I can get a taxi."

As I started to protest, she reached and pinched my cheek. "Haven't you discovered yet that I'm not one of those porcelain dolls? I don't like for people to hover anxiously over me. I prefer to run my own errands, do my own chores. I like to take care of myself."

She walked to the door. "Anyway," she added with a touch of a smile, "if you take me home, you might want to come up. And I might relent, right when I'm trying to be sore at you."

"Why be sore?"

"Because you are what you are," she said quietly. "No one or no force will ever change you until the day you die."

"Is that bad?"

"Sometimes. It was bad this evening. Some men would have felt they had a choice. But when you got the phone call, nothing or nobody could have kept you in this apartment."

"There wasn't really a choice, Myrtle. I had to go."

She tilted her head and studied me deeply. "You've made my point precisely, Ed."

"You're sounding a bit final, Myrtle."

"Am I? Chalk it up to my mood."

"Are you judging me?"

"Judging . . . ? Oh, no, Ed! No one has the right to judge another person. Seeing a human being clearly doesn't mean you're judging him. You're simply left alone in a place like this with the truth. You know that when next you hear of him, he will be dead—or he will have killed another man."

"Neither happened, Myrtle."

"A technicality," she said. "A twist of circumstance. All the forces and factors were there. The fullness of the truth and knowledge was driven home to me, you might say."

"You impressed me as a person big enough to face it."

"I don't know, Ed. I'm not sure of too many things right now. I need to sit in a taxi alone and later read a book with half of my mind while the half that really counts does some thinking. I need to get out of this aura of relentlessness that you somehow carry around with you. I . . . Good night, Ed. Call me in a couple of days."

She moved quickly, crossing the hallway, reaching the stair well, and sliding from view.

Eighteen

I closed the door slowly and leaned against it a moment. She had left a feeling of emptiness in the apartment, a shadowy stillness that was too conducive to unsettling thoughts.

I pushed away from the door and crossed to the telephone. I opened the book at the yellow pages. On the fourth call I made contact with a novelty shop that was open and that stocked what I was after. The place was in Ybor City, a few blocks from the apartment.

"Yes," a man's voice said, "we have a few pirate costumes left. What size do you need?"

"I'm a forty-two regular."

"I believe we can fix you up. Did you want the outfit tonight?"

"Yes."

"We were getting ready to close," he said.

I gave him my name and address. "I can come right over."

"Why don't I just drop it off? You're near by. I can go ahead and close and bring the costume on my way home."

"Fine," I said. "The apartment is on the second floor. I'll watch for you. One thing . . ."

"Yes?"

"Is there a beard with the outfit?"

"I can include one, Mr. Rivers."

"Big, bushy, to cover most of my face."

"Are you going to a masquerade?"

"Something like that," I said.

"I'll see that we come up with a suitable beard."

I worked on a beer while I waited. He arrived with a bulky suit box under his arm, a young, neat, dark-skinned man who probably operated the small shop with the part-time assistance of his wife.

He glanced me over, remarked that the costume should be perfect in size and that I was in luck. I handed over the rental fee and deposit money in exchange for a receipt and the cardboard box.

"The beard?" I asked as we stood in the apartment doorway.

"The most luxuriant one in the house," he said. "Very bushy. Very black. I also included a large black eye patch. Your disguise will be as effective as any at the masquerade."

"That's what I'm after," I assured him. "Thanks very much."

"No trouble, Mr. Rivers. Have fun."

"Sure," I said. "Always."

My tone brought a glance. *"Buenas noches."*

Alone in the apartment, I set the box on a table, flipped the tabs, and checked the contents. There were huge, baggy pantaloons of bright red to smother my bottom, and a short, skimpy jerkin to expose most of my lumpy torso to the evening breezes. Black oilcloth boots were designed to cover my shoe tops and strap under the instep. The turban was a brilliant blue, and there was a sash matching it in color. I fingered the eyepatch aside, picked up the beard and shook it out. It was a lulu.

I stripped to my shorts and climbed into the para-
phernalia.

With all the junk in place, I walked into the bathroom
for a final check of the mug in the medicine-cabinet
mirror.

I pulled the imitation silk turban a trifle lower on my
forehead. I was satisfied with the effect. Very little of the
original Ed Rivers showed through the montage of turban, eyepatch, and wild beard.

I paused once more, in the bed-sitting room, and
tucked the .38 under the waistband of the pantaloons
Only the blue sash remained. I wrapped it about my gut
to cover the butt of the gun. I didn't knot the sash to
let the ends dangle. I tucked in the ends so I could get
rid of the sash in a hurry.

As I left the apartment, I thought of the purpose and
meaning of Gasparilla. Festival. Fun week. And I was
on my way at last to a Gasparilla party . . .

When I came out of the building, the sky over the
Hillsborough River flashed with bursting bombs, falling
stars, and sputtering pinwheels of light. No kids were on
the street tonight; all were down by the river watching
the firewords display.

I got in the car, which I'd left at the curb, and eased
it into traffic. I didn't fight the tangle. But when I was
out to the vicinity where traffic thinned, I pushed the car.

I watched the boulevard lights swish past, slowed as I
neared the turnoff. A few minutes later, the car was picking its way along the driveway, through the jungle green-
ery of the estate of Señora Isabella. More correctly, the
showpiece of a twenty-million-dollar fortune that death
had earmarked for one Elena Sigmon.

I wedged the car behind a snooty little Porsche and

got out. The smell of hickory chips smoldering in the barbecue grills put a tang in the air. Beyond the vast lawn, the cozy glow of the paper lanterns beckoned romantically. The sounds of the tireless bongos and endlessly wailing saxophone drifted to me.

. As I walked across the lawn toward the hacienda, I concluded that the party was spreading out. I had to detour a couple who stood holding a long kiss, unaware of any other existence. Salome's gauzy veils swished about her as she ran teasingly across the lawn, looking over her shoulder at the lanky pirate who pursued her. She conveniently ran out of gas, laughing and gasping as he caught up with her. He scooped her up, and she stopped laughing as she put her lips against his.

I reached the end of the lawn. Nobody seemed to mind the additional pirate who wandered onto the courtyard.

I looked around the courtyard for Fred Eppling, Clavery, Natalie, and the Sigmons. I didn't see them, and decided they must be inside.

A little blond piratess had spotted me. As I started to move on, she weaved up, thrust a drink in my hand, and made an out-of-focus sound that resembled a hiccup crossed with a giggle.

"Wups!" She put her fingers over her mouth, looked at me dizzily, and staggered slightly. She got the giggle out by itself this time. "Getting a little drunk out . . . Look, everybody, Blackbeard himself!"

As I started around her, she came up with another giggle and stumbled between me and the house. She caught a tuft of the brown mat on my chest that was exposed by the jerkin. She tugged lightly. "Mister Mans, you're wired for sound!"

"Except my woofer is slightly on the blink."

The giggle became a shrill, stupid laugh. "That's barbed, that is." She jerked a few shreds of chest spinach right out of the garden. "You're the nearest thing to the real article at this blast. Do I know you?"

"I don't think so."

She reached up to give the beard a pull. I caught her wrist. "Naughty," I said. "That will never do."

"I want to know who you are," she pouted.

"Honey, I'm old José Gaspar come back from the briny deep to see if you're doing justice to my dedicated week."

"We're trying, José! We are really trying."

"I can see that."

"But who are you when you're not José Gaspar?"

I flicked her tip-tilted nose with my fingertip. "Part of the fun, lovely."

"I know what . . ." Her eyes became drunkenly sly. "I'll find out. I'll ask Keith who you are."

Deliver me, I thought, from the urge to bust such a nice young rump.

"Good idea," I said, wrenching a smile through the beard. "But you don't know where he is."

"Yes, I do, too. I do so know where Keith is!" She made a vague gesture toward the left wing of the house. "He's in there with Natalie Clavery."

"How about I find him for you?"

She brightened. "Okay."

"You wait right here."

"While I have a li'l ole drink." She hiccuped. "But you hurry back to Hildy."

"Sure, Hildy."

"Don't keep li'l Hildy waiting."

"Don't worry about a thing, Hildy."

I escaped blond little Hildy by fading into the shadows at the ell of the portico. I stopped short as the sound of someone being slapped with an open palm came to me from a few yards away.

I turned, not seeing them at first. Then I made out the shadowed forms of Van and Natalie Clavery standing under the portico. She was absolutely rigid, except for the hand she was raising slowly to her stinging cheek.

Clavery's wiry, intense body swayed under the assault of the emotion ripping through him. A strangled sound formed in his throat. His arms groped imploringly.

"Natalie . . ."

"No, don't say anything, Van. Don't make it worse by trying to apologize."

"I struck you, Natalie . . ."

"So you did, Van."

"I saw you in there with him, Natalie, with Keith Sigmon . . ."

"Were you spying, Van?"

"I wanted to kill him . . . of all men . . . Keith Sigmon. Then I saw Elena come in." Clavery was so filled with feeling he was unable to speak above a thick whisper. "I saw you start out . . . I waited . . . And when you stepped onto the portico . . . Before I knew what was happening, my hand was raising, swinging . . ."

"I think I'll go home, Van."

"No, no! Please. I think I know why you were in there."

"Do you, Van?"

"You think Keith and Elena have the old lady's missing portfolio, the confession I wrote out, the promissory note. Isn't that it? You thought it was the only way left to get the confession back. Tell me it's true, Natalie!"

"Do you believe it's true?" she asked him.

"Yes . . . . With a moment to think, I know it's true. You couldn't have any feeling for a man like Keith Sigmon, Natalie."

"Yes," she said, "I have feeling. I despise him."

"You'd despise me if I wanted, or even permitted, myself to be saved by that means," Clavery said. "I'd rather rot in jail."

"In any event, Van," she said with sudden weariness, "you haven't been saved. Elena came in before I had any chance to put my little last-stage plan in operation."

Nineteen

In the left wing of the solid old mansion the noise of the party was a rising and falling muffled wash of sound.

From the door through which I'd eased off the portico, I moved slowly along the hallway. At the distant end of this same hall were the same rooms I'd visited previously, rooms where the old *señora* and Jean Putnam had slept and worked. Much nearer to me, light spilled into the hall from a partially opened door.

The murmur of voices led me toward the lighted room. As I came closer, my view of the room's interior widened.

I heard Keith Sigmon say: "That's better. Cool off and listen to reason."

And Elena's voice: "Well, I did find you in here alone with Natalie Clavery."

Sigmon: "She's twice your age."

Elena: "You weren't acting like it."

My last step had carried me fully into the doorway. The room was a sort of combination den-library. The dark wood-paneled walls were lined with books. There was a fireplace of antique brick. Huge, comfortable couches and chairs graced the room. Tall French windows opened on a side lawn. Left of the windows was a well-stocked, tooled-leather bar.

Keith and Elena were in close contact, standing near an antique table on which a lamp glowed softly. He had one arm about her slender waist, pulling her tightly against him. With the fingertips of his other hand he was tipping her chin up, smiling and looking at her coaxingly.

"You're very impish when you pout," he said.

She began to relent. "I ought to claw your eyes out. You know that, don't you?"

"You'd miss me dreadfully," he said. "Anyway, it would all be for nothing. The Natalie Clavery bit didn't mean a thing, I tell you."

"It had better never repeat itself," she said.

"It won't," Sigmon promised.

He slid his hand to the back of her small head, laced his fingers through the light hair, and pulled the sharp prettiness of the little face forward. "This is the only thing worth repeating," he said softly. Then he kissed her, and with a soft sound in her throat, she responded.

I felt the tightness pull over my face, as if the skin had shrunk. I thought of the sickening shock a girl of Jean Putnam's caliber had experienced, chancing to look on a scene similar to this one. And after she'd crept away, face hot with the shame for them, Jean had begun asking herself questions. She'd started to look for answers, to inquire, to investigate. The questions had opened the area to bigger questions. And when the questions became demanding, Jean Putnam had sought a private detective to help her get the answers that would either clear these people or damn them.

Jean Putnam had been killed because she'd refused to let the questions lie unanswered. She'd unwittingly condemned Lura Thackery by writing in a diary the things she had seen and overheard, by putting the questions in Lura's possession.

It was that simple. The questions had the power to destroy—unless they were first destroyed.

With her dying breath, Jean Putnam had been trying to point to the very heart of the matter, the thing seen by chance that had raised the first question in her mind. She had not been trying to say the word "incense.' The word she formed in death was far uglier: "incest."

But the word comprised the question, not the answer. I spoke the answer with a soft hissing of breath: "Ginny . . . Ginny Jameson!"

Her involuntary response to her own name cleared any remaining doubt from my mind. The girl who'd posed as Elena Sigmon stood half turned in Keith Sigmon's arms, a sudden frightening knowledge killing the color of the pixie face.

As I moved toward them, Keith Sigmon released her, pushing her slightly to one side. The dissipated handsomeness of his face became old and hard, with a vicious old man's desire to live at whatever cost.

"Keith Sigmon and a slut of a call girl from Venezuela," I said. "Ginny Jameson, alias Elena Sigmon."

"Ed Rivers alias Blackbeard," Sigmon said thinly.

"Check."

"You . . . you don't know what you're talking about!" the girl said.

"I think so."

"A girl can kiss her daddy!"

"Not like that, honey. Neither does the sheltered granddaughter of a fine old Venezuelan family of aristocrats know how to dance the way you were dancing earlier. Your professional dancing experience was showing all over the place."

"That's no proof . . ."

"Venezuela is lousy with proof," I said. "All we've got to do is air-express a photograph over there and let people who knew you and Elena Sigmon have one look."

She lifted her arms and hugged herself. It didn't stop the shiver from crossing her shoulder.

Sigmon seemed incapable of movement, except at the lips. "Just what do you think happened, Rivers?"

"I know what happened," I said. "When she got the news that her grandmother had died in the States, your daughter, the real Elena, went up to the mountain cottage. To give you the news, Sigmon. She found the two of you there, and I imagine it was pretty sickening. It hit her hard, coming on top of news of her grandmother's death. No girl has probably ever felt more alone. She'd lost her grandfather and her mother to a terrorist's bomb. Her grandmother was lying dead in a distant land. And you, her father, were in the midst of an orgy with a slut.

"Demoralized by all that emotional dynamite, she

started down the mountain road recklessly. She never reached the final mile of the road. Her reactions failed at a curve. The car went over, caught fire.

"I imagine you were following her down, Sigmon. If you didn't see the actual crash, you saw the flames. In either event, you couldn't save her. How about it? Am I substantially correct? When the heat of the wreckage drove you back, I suppose even a louse like you had a moment of grief. Was the next part your idea or Ginny's?"

"It wasn't mine," Sigmon said in a suppressed voice.

Ginny's vixen face sharpened. "It didn't take much to talk you into it!"

"Of course not," I said. "Grief and remorse wouldn't bring Elena back. Her accidental death was an unalterable fact, a thing of the past. But it had a vital effect on the future. At stake was a twenty-million-dollar estate. When Elena died, the old *señora*'s vast assets would go in trust to charities and foundations.

"So why permit Elena to die? It seemed so simple at the time, didn't it, Sigmon? All you had to do was toss a few items belonging to the real Ginny into the burning wreckage, go to the police and report the death of Ginny Jameson—not the death of Elena Sigmon, heiress to a fabulous estate. You knew the investigation would be routine and brief. The Venezuelan authorities were glad enough to get Ginny Jameson off their hands. Later you picked up Ginny, boarded the plane with her as your daughter. Being an American by birth, you had no passport problem. With your type of friends in Caracas, I'm sure you had no trouble in obtaining any necessary changes and bits of forgeries in whatever papers Elena would need.

"It seemed quite clever, Sigmon. With Ginny waiting

under cover, probably at a hotel, you posed as the lone witness of the auto accident. Your word, uncontradicted, that it was Ginny Jameson who'd left the mountain cottage and crashed to her death.

"But a man can be too clever. I talked with Caracas. Not one time was Elena mentioned as being present during the investigation. You had to do it solo, giving them the impression you'd come down the mountain alone. You couldn't produce an Elena Sigmon to corroborate your story because there wasn't one still in the land of the living. This was an additional point, Sigmon, that steered me toward the truth."

He made a noise like a snuffling dog as he tried to get some moisture in his mouth. "All right," he said. "So you send a picture back to Caracas . . ."

"Keith!" Ginny said sharply.

He motioned her not to come nearer to him. "So I left my daughter in a desecrated grave," he said, the oldness growing in him. "I took a seat in a game for one of the world's fabulous fortunes." He laughed softly, briefly, bitterly. "Twenty million dollars . . . it still isn't worth dying for."

"Two young girls, Jean Putnam and Lura Thackery, paid a damned heavy price, Sigmon."

"But I didn't kill them. Neither did Ginny. Whatever happens, I intend to live. In jail. In the gutter. Anything beats dying—and you can't pin murder on me, Rivers."

"I know," I said. "I——"

The back of my head exploded. The carpet hit me in the face. The thick, plush nap ceased to exist for a few seconds, then returned to reality like stiff, stinging little barbs against my cheek.

Distantly, I heard Sigmon say, "You can't . . . I won't be a party to . . ."

"You've no choice now, darling," Ginny said with renewed brightness. "Let Rivers feed the fish in the bay and no one else will ever connect it up."

An expensive shoe pinned my knuckles against the carpet, and a third voice, male, said: "You were coming after me next, weren't you, Rivers?"

"Yes, Eppling. From here to you. I knew it all, once I got the final details in place."

"I thought so, when dear little Hildy started asking everyone who the big, black-bearded pirate stranger was," Fred Eppling said. "She really let the cat out for you, Rivers, when she said you were looking for Sigmon and had come in here. I decided it was time I came in quietly myself."

"Bless little Hildy," I said, "who surely deserves a twice-busted rump."

Twenty

The pressure of the shoe eased from my fingers. I turned slowly, sat up halfway, supporting myself with my palm against the carpet while my head endured a fresh blast of pain.

I raised my eyes slowly and saw the lawyer standing quietly over me, a small gun in his hand. Small, but quite capable of killing.

"For a bright lawyer with the lust for power and

wealth, the cold-blooded drive to tear himself out an education and start at the bottom of the heap in criminal law . . . for such a lawyer, Eppling," I said, "you pulled some bloopers. But maybe no human brain is smart enough to deal in murder—unless you're a totally brainless gunsel who contents himself in going out and knocking off other gunsels in gangland killings."

"Name me a blooper, Rivers."

"Sure," I said. "Always glad to oblige. Where shall I start? With Ben McJunkin? One of those pro killers who should have stayed with the mobs and mob killings. Just any citizen can't hire a guy like McJunkin, Eppling. How many ordinary working stiffs would even know how to go about hiring a murderer?

"Sigmon might have had some shady connections in Caracas who could have whispered a name in his ear. But neither he nor Ginny knew where to find a hired gun in Tampa. Van or Natalie Clavery? Nonsense. They wouldn't know where to start looking for a man like McJunkin.

"But you, Eppling . . . Everybody was ruled out but you. One-time small-peanuts criminal lawyer. A gunman in and out of Tampa for many years. It was a natural for you, Eppling, when you realized Jean Putnam had to be silenced.

"Want another blooper? Okay, serve up Keith Sigmon and Ginny Jameson. Keith could palm her off here as his daughter provided that no one here had ever seen the real Elena. Or—and this is how you cut yourself into a twenty-million-dollar gravy, Eppling—if anyone here who'd ever seen the real Elena would accept Ginny as a proxy."

"If you're trying to ring me in the middle of this thing,"

Sigmon burst out, "you're wrong. I never saw Fred Eppling until he met our plane."

"So you told me," I said. "But Myrtle Higgins let it slip that Fred Eppling made one trip to Caracas for the *señora* while the old lady was still alive. Mostly Eppling never had to do more than drop by the house here occasionally. But on that one trip, he would have met Elena, and you as well, Sigmon.

"Your instincts told you that you were two of a kind, greedy and ruthless. Before you could bring in Ginny as Elena, Sigmon, you had to make sure that Eppling, the lawyer handling the estate, would go for the deal. I'm sure we'll find a record of an overseas call when the cops start digging out and putting all the evidence and minor details together.

"Twenty million dollars was more than enough to go around, and when Eppling agreed to come in, the scheme got off to a flying start."

"But I never killed anybody," the old, hard man said. "It was Eppling who hired McJunkin, just as you say, Rivers. When Jean Putnam began to question us, I wanted to grab what was convenient for grabbing and make a run for it. Eppling wouldn't let me. He insisted that twenty million was too much to lose——"

"Even if I was fond of Jean," Eppling said quietly.

"Fond of her," I said, getting slowly to my feet. "Just more fond of twenty million smackers."

"I'm afraid that's the case," Eppling said. "You see . . . Jean came to me at the outset with her suspicions. Natural, I suppose, since I had been the *señora*'s lawyer and was handling the estate. I tried to dissuade Jean, convince her that her ideas were groundless. I was unable to do so. I had destroyed everything among the old *señora*'s personal things that might have pointed to the real Elena."

"Including that missing portfolio?" I said.

"Including the crummy old briefcase." Eppling's lips twisted. "Jean remembered there'd been some snapshots of the old *señora*'s family in the portfolio. She had reached the point where she wanted to see a picture of Elena. Jean . . . You see, she gave me no choice, Rivers."

"And Van Clavery's confession and promissory note?"

"In my office safe," Eppling said. "I planned to let them conveniently be found in some odd corner here in the house when things had quieted down."

"I think we've talked enough," Ginny said.

"Yes," Eppling said. "Of course. You're quite right, Ginny."

"Blackbeard . . . Blackbeard darling," sang a drunken little voice in the hallway. "You didn't keep your promise to come back . . . Where are you, Blackbeard?"

Hildy's sunny hair was a bright spot of color in the doorway. Keyed tight, the sound of her voice had brought a quiver and a glance from Eppling.

I went in under the the gun. With a snarl, Eppling swung it down, trying to slug me. The gun glanced off my back muscles as I hit him with my shoulder and carried him backward.

"Sigmon!" the word was jolted from Eppling as we hit the floor.

From the perimeter of my vision, I saw Sigmon's foot swinging at me. I ducked, grappling with Eppling for the gun.

Hildy started screaming.

Sigmon piled on me and Ginny joined the fray with

fingernails reaching for my eyes. I'd half risen, holding Eppling's wrist. The bunch of us hit the floor in a writhing mass.

I felt Sigmon being yanked off me as the summons of Hildy's scream was answered. I got an impression of Van Clavery using those tense, wiry muscles behind a small, hard fist. I heard Sigmon crash into a table, make kindling of it, and roll to the floor, an unconscious old man.

Eppling was trying to knee me in the groin and writhe from beneath me while Ginny kicked at my kidneys. Holding onto that gun hand, I took a second to grab her ankle and jerk her feet from under her.

While I had the hand free, I doubled it and stuck it in the side of Eppling's face. My fist glanced off his cheekbone. He quit trying to rupture me with his knees. I stood, dragging him up with me. With his left he swung a roundhouse. I blocked it, got punching room, and aimed one straight at his nose.

My aim was good. His eyes rolled up. His knees folded, and he dangled from my grip by his gun wrist.

I let him slide to the floor and picked up the small gun where it had fallen from his fingers.

"Ginny," I said.

She drew to a stop short of the door where sunny Hildy stood. She turned slowly, saw the gun, the wreckage in the room. She went gropingly to a chair, sat down, pressed her knees tightly together, and stared at nothing, at sheer emptiness. At her future, possibly.

"Catch," I said to Clavery, pitching him Eppling's small gun.

"I don't think there's time for a long explanation right now. So get this. Keep this trio covered. She's not

Elena Sigmon. She's Ginny Jameson. It was a twenty-million-dollar hoax that didn't quite pan out, even though Eppling hired Ben McJunkin as a long-reaching weapon. Get the cops and tell them to get with Caracas while they start a third-degree on these creeps. I'll report in at headquarters as soon as possible, but they can tie up the Putnam-Thackery case, now that they knew where to start the knots."

"Rivers——"

"Later," I said. "Your note and confession are in Eppling's safe."

"How could Fred have——"

"For a slice of a twenty-million-dollar estate," I said. "Now for cripe's sake, can you do as I ask?"

"Of course," he said quietly. The gun was steady, quite deadly in his high-strung, capable hand.

The ruckus had proved too much for Hildy. She had made herself scarce. I'd probably never have the chance to apologize for the destructive thoughts I'd had in regards to her very nice little rump.

A bigger, more lush, far more female woman than Hildy opened her door to me a short time later. She stood there looking at me, the light behind her spilling through the mane of dark-blond hair.

"Aren't you going to ask me in, Myrtle?"

"I'm really tired, Ed. Like I told you . . . a good book is my present limit, as fetching as your costume is."

"I want Ben McJunkin, Myrtle."

"What makes you think——"

"It all adds up." I pushed into the small living room of her apartment and looked at the open suitcases she'd been packing. An emptiness began to fan out inside of me. "Packing your books too?"

"Ed . . ."

"No," I said. "Let's not talk about it. I understand now. You almost fainted when I returned from the San Salvador Hotel. But not from relief. It was because my return meant I might have killed him. You did it all for him, didn't you? Sticking close. As close as a bedsheet, if necessary, to keep tabs on his enemy, to help him in any way you could. When did you first meet him, Myrtle?"

"A long time ago . . . in an emergency ward . . . I was on duty. They brought him in one night. A colored fellow had cut him all to pieces, but he refused to die . . . He was too tough, too much a man to die like that."

She walked to the window and watched the starshells burst over the river. "I don't suppose anyone would understand," she said after a moment. "He never married me. He was restless and would be gone a large part of the time. But he always came back. Nothing else was more important. From the time he met a green kid wearing her first nurse's uniform, he always came back."

"For whatever he needed," I said. "If it was medical attention he had a fine trained nurse—while the cops checked all the doctors for a wounded man."

"Is that what put you onto me?" she asked quietly.

"Your hurry to leave my apartment tonight and get to him clinched it," I said. "There were other things. The size of the garments in McJunkin's hotel room. The fact that Jean Putnam kept a diary, a fact a co-worker of Jean's would know and could relay to McJunkin.

"I know now it was you, Myrtle, trying to call him right after I slipped into his room. You weren't able to warn him; so you tipped his principal, Fred Eppling, that I'd located McJunkin's address. Only you could have done that, Myrtle. Only you knew I'd discovered where McJunkin was staying. I'm sure you thought Eppling would head McJunkin off, warn him. Instead, Eppling had no choice but to start shooting at me through McJunkin's window.

"Then there was a statement you made in my apartment, Myrtle, when I told you the fingerprint on my doorknob belonged to a man named McJunkin. Almost immediately, you used the full name. *Ben* McJunkin. It went over my head at the time. When the parts shaped up, I remembered."

She had the attitude of listening for a cry from some great distance or a whisper in the nearby darkness. After a long, long moment, she seemed to remember I was there. She made a little motion toward the open suitcases. "All my things, Ed. None of his."

"Where is he, Myrtle?"

She looked through the window to the endless dark skies. The Gasparilla stars had all quit falling. The party was over. The skies were totally black.

"Where?" she said. She looked at the floor. I followed her glance, saw the still-damp places where she had tried to scrub the traces of blood from the carpet.

I turned my head to look at the bedroom door. My hand dropped to the gun beneath the blue pirate's sash.

"No, Ed . . ." she said in a tone beyond grief. "You can open the door. You won't need the gun. He managed to get here, but he was beyond help. You killed him, Ed . . . back there at the San Salvador Hotel."

I looked at her, and I believed her. I felt empty and slightly defeated. My lips were very dry. I touched them with the wetness of my tongue, and said "Ben McJunkin,

Myrtle . . . when you could have had any man. After all these years, still Ben McJunkin . . . Why?"

She looked past me, thinking of the years, picking out and recalling the individual hours that lived in her memory. For the barest fraction of a second, Myrtle Higgins wasn't incomplete. The power of her feeling changed her. And I glimpsed beyond the two dimensional physical surface that she had always presented to me or any other man—except one.

I would remember what I had seen for a long time.

The longhairs with degrees papering their walls can study it a lifetime and write a library of books about it. They'll never have her knowledge of it. To Myrtle Higgins it was very simple. Right or wrong, for good or for evil, she expressed it all and told the whole tale in three words.

"I loved him," she said.